VOICES FROM THE BIALYSTOK GHETTO

VOICES FROM THE BIALYSTOK GHETTO

Including the Diary of David Spiro, a Young Victim

Michael Nevins

Voices From the Bialystok Ghetto
Including the Diary of David Spiro, a Young Victim

iUniverse books may be ordered through booksellers or by contacting:

iUniverse
1663 Liberty Drive
Bloomington, IN 47403
www.iuniverse.com
1-800-Authors (1-800-288-4677)

ISBN: 978-1-5320-8864-3 (sc)
ISBN: 978-1-5320-8865-0 (e)

Print information available on the last page.

iUniverse rev. date: 12/12/2019

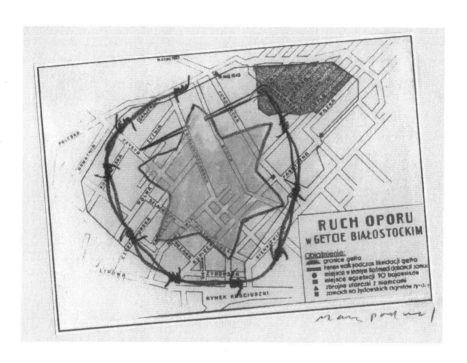

Including the War Diary of David Spiro, a Young Victim

*History is written from what can be found; what isn't saved is
lost, sunken and rotted, eaten by earth.* (Jill Lepore, 2014)

Dedicated to the many splendid ethnic Poles who
are working to preserve and honor the memory
of their country's lost Jewish community.

CONTENTS

INTRODUCTION

My paternal grandparents Hyman Neviadomsky and Celia Zaban grew up in Dabrowa, a *shtetl* in czarist Russia nearly forty miles northeast of Bialystok. They immigrated to New York City during the 1890s where they married and spawned four children who, in turn, were fruitful and multiplied. The family's surname was changed to the Yankee-sounding Nevins, but I neither knew (nor cared) about any of this until, when in my early forties, I became interested in our roots. By then my grandparents were long gone but I was able to interview several relatives and *landsmen* and in 1982 published a memorial book about Dabrowa Bialostocka's lost Jewish community. A dozen years later I first visited the town (now located in northeastern Poland) when, with others from around the world, I participated in a dedication ceremony in the partially restored Jewish cemetery.

Another decade passed when I received an unexpected invitation to speak at a conference that was planned to be held in Dabrowa Bialostocka in May 2016. It was organized by Dorata Budzinska, a local school teacher who engages her students in studying their town's Jewish history and, of course, I accepted. On that memorable occasion the simultaneous translator of my speech was Elzbieta Smolenska, a photojournalist who grew up in Bialystok and now lives in England. Afterward the two of us remained in contact and in April 2019, when I had occasion to meet Elzbieta in London, she surprised me with a gift.

It was the recently published diary of a young Bialystoker, David Spiro who was nearing age eighteen when he began writing in 1939. (I choose to use the common English spelling for what in Polish is spelled Dawid

Szpiro. An alternate version of the surname could be Shapiro.) David's hometown had recently been occupied by the Russian army who two years later would be displaced by the Nazis. The last of 52 diary entries was made on July 12, 1943, several weeks before Bialystok's destruction, and then the narrative abruptly ended. The reader can only guess at the author's fate. Why David's diary lay virtually unnoticed for more than seven decades remains unclear, but it was about to be discarded with trash when someone looked inside and discerned its historic value.

The crude document was purchased by the Slendzinsky Gallery in Bialystok and published there in August 2018 as *Pamiętnik* (Diary) with accompanying English translation and commentaries. When introduced at a memorial event for the 75th anniversary of the Bialystok Ghetto Uprising, the city's mayor Tadeusz Truskolaski declared, "Anyone who identifies with our city…who wants to get to know our roots better, should read this publication…It is worth lending an ear to the voice of the murdered community…Let us cherish the memory of our heritage, let us save this story from oblivion."

Pamiętnik is the only contemporaneous account of life in the Bialystok ghetto that has been fully translated from Polish to English and, as such, serves as a riveting shard from that vanished world. It portrays the coming of age of a callow post-adolescent who, unlike Anne Frank whose famous diary was written while she was in hiding, was out in the streets confronting the daily horror of occupation. In early entries David described playing endless games of poker, drinking vodka with friends, missing female company - sometimes even being "bored." While today some of his experiences may seem banal, others were terrifying. Indeed, if David Spiro had a "cause" it was to do whatever he could to survive, even if it meant serving for a time as a despised Jewish "policeman" in the ghetto.

1

Testimonies

Amidst the vast genre of Holocaust literature memoirs enable readers to confront the human dimension of the catastrophe. Often written long after the fact, sometimes they fail to capture the immediacy of events and may be distorted by the survivor's knowledge of related or subsequent history. Conversely, personal diaries permit the reader to identify with the solo voice of an eye-witness speaking to them as if in real time. Professor Sherry Turkle of M.I.T. suggests that the diary is "a human-paced experience of how someone's mind works and how their ideas unfold. Such prolonged engagement in another person's thinking produces empathy, a quality in short supply these days." (*Smithsonian Magazine*, November 2018.)

Alexandra Zapruder is a scholar who starting in 1991 as a novice research assistant at the still incomplete United States Holocaust Museum, began gathering the diaries of dozens of young victims. In 2002 she published an anthology *Salvaged Pages: Young Writers' Diaries of the Holocaust* (later she co-produced a documentary film based on the same material, *I'm Still Here.*) For more than two decades she travelled widely making diverse audiences aware that Anne Frank's was not the only voice that personalized the nature and effects of hatred and intolerance during the Second World War.

Alexandra Garbarini is another academic whose book *Numbered Days* (2006) was based on roughly one hundred Holocaust diaries, most of them written in Polish. In her preface Garbarini noted, "I aim to make it possible to see diarists as active subjects in history - not as passive victims or heroic resisters, but as ordinary men and women who were subjected to extraordinary events and who tried in different ways to cope with them." Taken together these snapshots create a composite that provides the reader with an unmediated understanding of the Holocaust.

A stark example of this genre was another long-hidden war diary written by Renia Spiegel, a precocious teenager who lived in Przemysl, a small city in southern Poland and began writing when she was fifteen. In her first entry (September 31, 1939) Renia explained:

> *Why did I decide to start my diary today? Did something important happen? Have I discovered that my friends are keeping diaries of their own? No! I just want a friend. I want somebody I can talk to about my everyday worries and joys. Somebody who will feel what I feel, believe what I say and never reveal my secrets. No human being could ever be that kind of friend and that's why I have decided to look for a confidant in the form of a diary.*

Renia Spiegel continued for more than three years and some 700 pages until she was discovered hiding in an attic with family members and murdered on the spot. Her diary was retrieved by a boyfriend who decades later delivered it to her younger sister Arianna who'd been saved by a family friend and brought up Catholic. As an adult she (now Elizabeth Bellak) moved to New York City and stored her sister's diary in a safe-deposit box in a Manhattan bank - too painful to read. It finally was published in Polish in 2016, an English translation followed the next year in *Smithsonian Magazine* and in September 2019 *Renia's Diary* was published in full, sold in bookstores in more than a dozen countries and made widely available on the internet.

David Spiro was not the only witness who described events in Bialystok. Indeed, as journalist Masha Gessen has suggested, "it seems virtually every survivor of the Bialystok ghetto has written a memoir." Gessen's own contribution *Two Babushkas* told the stories of her two grandmothers who survived the war, one of whom, Ester Goldberg, grew up in Bialystok in a relatively affluent family; her mother was an active Bundist (socialist), her father a banker and ardent Zionist. In August 1940 the 16 year old left to study at a college in Moscow, but her father Jakub Goldberg remained in Bialystok where he served on the *Judenrat* (Jewish council) and died during the ghetto uprising. Masha Gessen's book provides authentic detail about her grandmother's early life in Bialystok, but during the worst war years under Nazi rule grandmother Ester was in Moscow so that the narrative lacks some of the raw emotion of a first-hand account such as David Spiro's diary.

Another young Bialystoker Lena Jedwab also wrote a diary (*Girl with Two Landscapes.The Wartime Diary of Lena Jedwab 1941*-1945) but like Ester Goldberg, was away from her hometown during the war years. Her family were Marxists and during the summer of 1939, the teenager was sent to a summer camp for Communist Pioneers in Lithuania. Three weeks later when Germany invaded Poland, Lena was moved to a remote area in Russia where she was stranded and never able to return to Bialystok. The following two entries illustrate the despair of this bright girl who was separated from her family and her city:

November 26, 1941

> *What will be in the future? When will the war end? When will I finally be able to go home? When will I be able to see my parents, my family, my friends? I write their first and family names on the cover of my notebook. Life is gray, dark...I yearn for the excitement of the big city, for our culture, for a good book, a good play, movie or concert, for our community, for our interesting life! Who has the right to deny me my wishes?*

November 28, 1941

> *It's half a year already that I'm away from home - half a year in which I haven't seen a Yiddish book, newspaper*

or journal. I long for Yiddish literature, to see Yiddish in print....The thought that I may have to spend long years in this environment, that I'll forget Yiddish more and more makes me sad...Tomorrow is my birthday - seventeen years old. The most beautiful years of a person's life. For me, they are lost; joy is forbidden....Mama! Is she alive? Who in my family is alive? And if they are alive, do they still remember the date of my birthday?

Although Lena Jedwab was fluent in Polish and Russian, she chose to write in Yiddish. She survived the war, eventually married and moved from Moscow to Paris and late in life began transcribing her diaries into publishable form, the work finally completed and translated by her daughter.

After the end of World War II when the enormity of the catastrophe was realized, more than six hundred *landsmanshaftn* (home town societies) published so-called *yizkor* books - multi-authored histories of the communities from where they or their families originated. Among them was *The Bialystoker Memorial Book (Der Bialystoker yisker-bukh)* published in English and Yiddish in 1982 by The Bialystok Center in Manhattan and several passages from it are contained herein. In addition, many personal accounts and historical reviews can be found on internet websites (e.g. zchor.org/Bialystok, JewishBialystok.pl or BIALYgen.)

Bialystok's fate was representative of many towns in Eastern Europe, but unlike most others a large documentary record was left. A comprehensive review *The Jews of Bialystok during World War II and the Holocaust* was written by Israeli historian Sara Bender who had access to both primary and secondary material not available to English-only readers until a translation of her book appeared in 2008. Among memoirs written by former residents some of which will be discussed later were *The Underground Army* by Chaika Grossman; *Of Blood and Hope* by Samuel Pisar; *Stories Our Parents Found Too Painful To Tell Us* by Rafael Rajzner (English translation by Dr. Henry Lew) and *Angel of the Ghetto* by Sam Solasz. Books written by descendants of Bialystok survivors included *Needle and Thread: A Tale of Survival from Bialystok to Paris* (experiences of Charles "Shleimah" Zabuski as told to his daughter June Brott) and *Jewels and Ashes* written by Arnold Zable, a grandson of survivors. Books of related general interest were *Jewish Bialystok and Surroundings in Eastern Poland: A Travel Guidebook* by Tomasz Wisniewski, *Jewish Bialystok and Its Diaspora* by Rebecca Kobrin and Mimi Sheraton's charming *The Bialy Eaters: The Story of a Bread and a Lost World*.

In contrast to David Spiro's experience in Bialystok, two diarists in the Warsaw Ghetto, Emmanuel Ringelblum and Chaim Kaplan, were men with a mission. Ringelblum formed a clandestine group of about two dozen men and women known as *Oyneg Shabes* (Joy in the Sabbath) and encouraged members to gather all manner of documents. As historian Samuel Kassow noted (p. 208), "In good times and bad, Polish Jewry spoke in many different voices; the men and women of the *Oyneg Shabes* did all they could to record those voices and ensure their survival until someday someone would listen." These materials were buried in ten metal boxes and two milk cans, a first cache hidden in August 1942 at the height of the Great Deportation, followed by another in February 1943 not long before the Ghetto Uprising broke out. One trove was unearthed shortly after the war while a second was discovered in December 1950; a probable third cache was never found.

Chaim Kaplan could have secured an exit visa, but felt obliged to remain in order to record events during the occupation. To write everything down was a self-appointed "sacred task," as if bearing witness to the suffering of Warsaw's Jewry spiritually sustained him. Every day he added to what he called his "scroll of agony" filling a notebook of 200 to 400 pages roughly every six months. Kaplan wrote, "We are so tired. There is no strength left to cry; steady and continual weeping finally leads to silence. At first there is screaming; then wailing; and at last a bottomless sigh that does not leave an echo. We live broken and shattered lives." Another time: "my mind is still clear though it is now five days since any real food has passed my lips."

Friends urged the sixty year old Chaim Kaplan to stop writing: "What is the purpose? How will these words of yours reach future generations?" But he refused to listen. Kaplan knew that events recorded in reportorial style can be of historical value and although he acknowledged that it was beyond his capabilities to describe every event in organized form, he hoped that others would do this when the appropriate time came. Chaim Kaplan's diaries were not hidden in Ringelblum's underground archive, but separately buried by a family friend on a farm outside the ghetto and retrieved after the war.

Although both Emmanuel Ringelblum and Chaim Kaplan died in the Warsaw Ghetto their words did reach future generations and now, before we "listen to the voices" of several citizens of Bialystok, a brief review of the city's Jewish history should provide helpful context.

2

A Short History of Jewish Bialystok

During the late 18th century, as a result of partitions by its avaricious neighbors Prussia, Austria and Russia, Poland's territory was divided into three parts. After 1795 the country entirely disappeared from the geopolitical map as an independent entity and for the next 123 years, until the end of World War I, the country's former eastern region was part of Czarist Russia. For a brief period between the world wars, Poland was reconstituted as a nation - the so-called Second Republic - but after the end of World War II it became a satellite of the Soviet Union until achieving full independence in 1989.

Jews first settled in the Bialystok region in the mid-17th century and their numbers steadily grew until during the early 20th century the city had the densest Jewish population of any in Eastern Europe. From 1900 to 1939 Jews numbered between 40,000 and 60,000 people, at various times constituting 50 to 75% of a general population of nearly 100,000. During World War II almost all of the city's Jews were killed and today, in this entirely rebuilt city of nearly 300,000, hardly any admit to even having Jewish roots.

During the 19th century Bialystok transformed from a small town to an industrial center producing cloth, linen, silk and tobacco. In 1895 when there were 230 textile factories the city was called the "Manchester of the North." At one time more than three quarters of the factories were owned by Jewish entrepreneurs. People of all ethnicities from small surrounding communities were drawn into an industrial vortex; as one historian wrote, "the lure of the factory, of an expanding city, could no longer be resisted. A family needs bread, work, prospects for a better life."

Bialystok became noted for its educational, charitable, medical and social organizations. It also was a center of the revolutionary labor movement with competing factions: socialists (the Bund), communists, Zionists, anarchists. The city was the birthplace of Dr. Ludwig Zamenhof, the eye doctor who created the international language Esperanto, and of Max Weber the famous cubist painter. Albert Sabin, the discoverer of the oral polio vaccine was born there, native son Yitzhak Shamir became the seventh prime minister of Israel and archeologist Yigal Yadin rose to chief of staff of the Israeli army. However, the overwhelming majority of Bialystok's Jews were neither rich or famous; most were poor factory workers and humble shopkeepers.

Amidst the first Russian Revolution, a pogrom erupted in June 1906 led by hooligans who were abetted by policemen and soldiers. The massacre lasted for three days, sidewalks were covered with blood, at least 88 Jews murdered and close to 700 wounded. Russian authorities intended to rule and divide by fostering hatred between Poles and Jews and other ethnic groups who opposed the Czar. A rumor was spread that a Jewish terrorist had shot the Bialystok police chief so that violence was justifiable - Christian vengeance against Jewish terror. Although many Poles didn't participate or sheltered Jews, this pogrom, and a smaller one the previous year, prompted many people to question the safety of remaining and tens of thousands immigrated to Western Europe, Argentina, Australia and North America - especially to the Lower East Side of New York City.

Nevertheless, during the interwar period, Bialystok thrived and the Jewish community had more synagogues per capita than any city in the world. There were numerous schools, orphanages, old age homes, an ambulance service and multiple charities that earned it the reputation, "The City with the Golden Heart." All of that came to an end after September 1 1939 when the war began.

At noon on the second day of Rosh Hashanah (September 15, 1939) the first German divisions arrived on Bialystok's deserted streets, firing flame-throwers through windows into homes and stores. Hundreds were killed or wounded in the first assault. The Wehrmacht occupied Bialystok for one week before, according to terms of the secret Molotov–Ribbentrop non-aggression pact, they turned authority over to the Soviet Union. When the Red Army arrived on Yom Kippur, the Jewish populace said prayers of gratitude that they'd been granted a reprieve - the lesser of two evils. They were greeted with flowers and speeches, red flags flew and the town clock was reset to Moscow time. Many young people were swept up with communist propaganda and welcomed the promise of a better future. The communists proclaimed "Everything for the workers" but then added, "Hebrew teachers are no good. Zionists are no good." Although the euphoria didn't last for long, Bialystok's Jewish community learned to adapt.

To be sure, the Soviet period was a difficult time for all groups and in some respects the NKVD were as bad as the Gestapo. A majority of some 450,000 citizens of Eastern Poland who were deported to Siberia and Kazakstan were ethnic Poles - in addition to Ukrainians, Byelorussians, Gypsies and Jews. For nearly two years conditions were relatively calm and as Bialystok became a haven for refugees fleeing Nazi-occupied areas, the population more than doubled. When the Germans turned against their erstwhile allies in June 1941, many people fled with the Red Army or made their way to the East as best they could.

Immediately upon entering Bialystok on June 27 the Germans burned the Great Synagogue to the ground with roughly one thousand Jews locked inside -estimates of those killed varied between 800 and 2,000. Most were men but some women and children also were crammed inside and only a scant few escaped through a back door. As one witness recalled, "Dante's pictures from Hell could be seen in the streets." From everywhere, wretched groups were led to the burning Great Synagogue and from within could be heard heartbreaking screams. The Germans forced their victims to push one another into the burning synagogue and those who refused were shot, their bodies thrown in. The death machine worked smoothly with precision and inhuman cruelty.

Soldiers threw hand grenades into the wooden houses which easily caught fire and soon the entire area was in flames.The inferno blazed for days and entire streets disappeared into mountains of ash. The sound of exploding grenades mingled with gunshots, shouts of drunken Germans and cries of the victims. During the following weeks thousands more were executed with 6,000 shot and buried in a mass grave at the city's northern edge.

3

The Ghetto

On August 1, 1941 a walled ghetto with three gates was formed to contain between 40 and 60,000 people - the number expanding and contracting as migrants were brought in from surrounding towns while simultaneous on-site killing and mass deportations emptied the overcrowded space. David Spiro couldn't believe what he was witnessing and wondered, "A ghetto in the 20th Century?"

The Bialystok ghetto was divided into two parts, on the east and west sides of the Biala River. It quickly became an industrial center where textiles and weapons were manufactured for the Germans. Most of the Jews worked in these industries while a few worked in German factories outside the ghetto. Within this setup, the Jews also managed to secretly manufacture products for their own use and because the Germans gave the Jews very little to eat, they grew their own vegetables in *"Judenrat* gardens."

The *Judenrat* set up soup kitchens, two hospitals, outpatient clinics, two schools, a court. A semblance of law and order was supervised by about 200 Jewish "policemen" who were charged with preventing illegal gatherings, ensuring public cleanliness, fighting crime, guarding the gates and fences and punishing those who disobeyed orders. Although the police were reluctant to participate in the most onerous actions demanded by their Gestapo masters, to refuse would result in them being shot.

Starting on July 12 nearly 5,000 Jews were executed in Pietrasze Forest, 2 km north of the city, and buried in a mass grave. That Fall about 4,500 of the sick, unskilled and unemployed or those who didn't have patrons in the *Judenrat* were deported from Białystok's ghetto to one in Prużany (two years later when that ghetto was liquidated, some 10,000 Jews either were murdered or shipped to Treblinka or Auschwitz.) For those remaining in Bialystok life was hard, sometimes brutal, and all had to fight for existence. The outlying districts had been "purged" - made *judenrein* - and Ephraim Barasch, the leader of the *Judenrat,* realizing the imminent peril said, "We must find ways of preventing, or at least curtailing, the danger. Unfortunately for us, Bialystok has recently become the largest ghetto after Lodz. The enemy has us in its sights. Now, only a miracle can avert the danger."

In November 1942 underground leaders sent 24 year old Mordecai Tenenbaum to Bialystok to join a dozen members of *Dror,* one of the Zionist youth groups. (Mordecai's surname often is hyphenated Tenenbaum-Tamaroff because he employed a Polish Tatar alias Josef Tamaroff.) The activists' purpose was to unite discordant factions in the ghetto and organize resistance, but when the group arrived from Vilna they were surprised by the passivity of the local young people. As one of them recalled, "What a marvelous youth Bialystok had. But how devoid of foresight! We undertook the task of bringing the gospel of the [*Dror*] Movement to them. We wanted to deprive this youth of its complacency, to shock it into disquiet."

At the end of January 1943, rumors spread that the *Judenrat* had received an order from the Gestapo to create a list of 12,000 Jews, ostensibly for work assignments. The activists feverishly prepared for armed resistance. Agents were sent out to obtain weapons and a large quantity of acid was distributed among the more daring Jewish women to hurl in the faces of the Nazis should they attack. It became known that the *Judenrat* had secretly compiled the lists but didn't want to cause panic. Tragedy lurked and the mood became agonizingly tense.

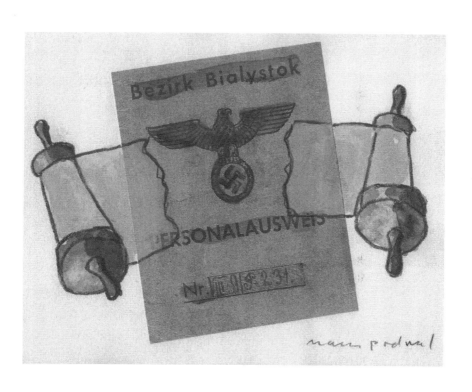

4

A Lone Voice: David Spiro's
War Diary *Pamietnik*

David Spiro's diary described life in the Bialystok area from the perspective of an ordinary young man. He was an assimilated Jew from a rather well-to-do family, certainly not a charismatic leader and it's difficult to imagine him being one of the martyred fighters during the ghetto uprising. No one encouraged David to keep a diary; indeed, in one entry he mused, "If someone reads my diary in the future, will they be able to believe something like that? Surely not, they will say poppycock and lies; but this is the truth, disgusting and terrible; for me it's a reality which I would like to avenge so much."

What follows next, reproduced with the permission of the diary's owner the Slendzinsky Gallery, are slightly edited excerpts from an English translation of the document that originally had been written in Polish.

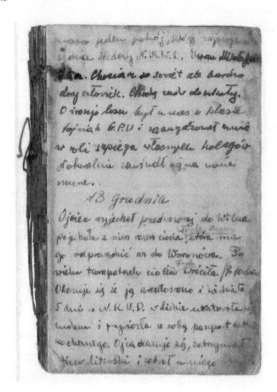

December 18, 1939

Father left for Vilnius two days ago....As it turned out he was stopped by a Lithuanian officer who took everything from him...My poor dad, he must have suffered so much. I would like to be with him, maybe one day I will go....In recent days those wretches and bandits came to take the furniture, mommy cried - the poor, ill woman. They took my motorcycle as well (damn them all to hell.) I must stop writing now because I might just lose my mind. I don't do anything. I dropped from school because they insulted me and called me "bourgeois." I can't do anything because I'm the son of a factory owner as if I have the plague. I play cards with my friends all day who are as unhappy as I am....Among the "Reds" I need to pretend that the Soviets make me happy and that I am naturally a communist, but this is hard for me. God, please end it because I'm so exhausted.

The roughly two year period under Russian rule was relatively orderly compared to the Nazi horror that soon would follow. Nevertheless, there were deportations and imprisonments, privatization of businesses and factories, seizure of private property and a daily struggle for food and clothing and Jews were not the only ones victimized. David and his mother were moved to nearby and safer Suprasl because in Bialystok he was known as a "son of a bourgeois."

March 3, 1940

> *Today is my birthday. I'm now finishing my 18th year. The first birthday I celebrate alone without my mommy and daddy. Daddy is far away…I got a message that he arrived safe and sound in Vilnius. He is so happy that there is no Bolshevik "freedom" there…The winter was terrible this year, the temperature in Bialystok -35C. Thank God, the war in Finland ended. USSR disgraced itself completely. The small Finnish nation was able to resist the 200 million Soviet Union. They start once again to deport bourgeoise, kulaks [land owners], and intelligentsia to Archangel. This month we are supposed to receive Soviet passports.*

March 10, 1940

> *They have deported almost all of my friends. Everyone tries to save themselves any way they can. Me and my mommy, we sleep on packed bags ready for travel… We did not get the passports. I'm starting to look for a job. Maybe they will accept me at the chauffeur's school but I highly doubt it. Many intelligent and rich women sank very low. Their husbands were deported or arrested and now they mess*

around with commanders and NKVD officers so they can remain here for the time being.

March 26, 1940

The Soviet newspapers are so stupid, nothing to read inside, only some nonsense about "freedom" in Russia...When you read the newspaper you get the impression that USSR, despite its friendship with Germany, actually sides with the Allies. Money is almost gone. There is no way to earn anything...Lizka Sokolowska is not in as dire a situation and she does not abandon me, supports me, and is with me almost the entire time. I have hidden many of our belongings from being "liberated" at her place.

April 6, 1940

The Germans have started a rapid offensive on France through Belgium and the Netherlands.....I think that soon we will leave our old apartment, but the tragedy is that they don't want to give us a new one. I visited Uncle Szmul, my good old uncle, how he loves daddy and mommy! He cried when he saw me.

May 21, 1940

They dismantled the town hall in the winter - the city's historic memento from the times of Napoleon. In place of the former town square they built a monument to those fallen in the fight for "freedom and communism." With great trouble we managed to get a transition room. I got a job as a gardener. The work is quite hard because for 8 hours I have to dig dirt and carry rubble. My boss is a very good man, a Polish patriot and an ardent enemy of the Soviets. Thanks to him I got a slightly better job. I am currently a foreman.

June 1, 1940

I spend my days following radio reports on the progress of the German offensive in France. I can't understand these events at all. How come the Frenchmen, Belgians, Dutchmen and Englishmen allow Germans to beat them so hard? The German offensive is now heading toward Dunkirk but I think that they will not get there, and maybe they will face a proper resistance.

There is a belief that soon there will be a German-Soviet war, although currently their relations are as good as they can be....I feel danger in the air. From what I have heard I gather that me and my mother will be sent to the "white bears" [Siberia.]

Money is running out, we are selling what remains of our possessions, prices are extremely high, there are queues for everything. Everyone is being constantly spied on, every other person has become an NKVD agent. I miss daddy terribly. Oh how it hurt when we sat down for Seder without him and without the traditionally prepared table......Each letter from daddy is read over and over again until it falls apart.

In my short life I have already been a student, a gardener, a manager, a menial worker and now for a change I am a metalworker and a mechanic [working in the factory formerly owned by his father.] *A truly Ford-like career and the jumps and adventures for Wells or Conan Doyle's novel. In my free time I took up playing cards again...Once a week I march to Bialystok* [from Suprasl, a small town about 16 km. away] *to see Lizka. Only now I realize how much I love her because when she is not with me I miss her terribly.*

August 5, 1940

I changed profession once again. Now I am an electro-mechanic for a change. I am as much an electrician as "a hammer is a nose."....In general: boredom, boredom, and even more boredom. I think about ways to get to Bialystok [to see Lizka.] There is no political news and there is little hope that the war will end soon.

September 15, 1940

Hungry for women and fun. Vodka flows like tap water because there is nothing else to do....Lizka visits quite often, almost every Saturday. I go to Bialystok from time to time but I'm afraid that someone will stop me and check my papers and then I will go to prison for a year, as I am not allowed to leave Suprasl. I feel as if I'm slowly being overgrown with moss in this parochial hole and I can't do anything about it. I have to sit tight and keep quiet. I've heard that General Sikorsky spoke and said "that on Christmas Eve we will break bread at home," but I don't believe that.

September 17, 1940

There was a letter from daddy, he is leaving for Kaunas and from there he plans to go further. They are trying to get papers. **1** *Supposedly upon arriving in Vilnius they opened a cotton wool factory but were smoked out by the Bolsheviks. Uncle Iser, Jaglom and others have already left for Shanghai...If only I could reach him [father].*

September 27, 1940

Mommy got very sick, her whole left side became paralyzed, from head to her leg. I work the night shift at the factory and a fireman came running to me to say that the director is giving me a free day. I immediately rushed home where I met two doctors and a feldsher [paramedic]. They concluded that her state is hopeless because there are no appropriate resources and the paralysis is progressing...

Lizka went to B-stok to fetch a doctor [but] the son of a bitch Doctor Prylucki, who was taking care of my mother the entire time, refused to come. Two hours later Doctor Abram Kohan came in his military machine. He gave my mother a shot of glucose and performed some other medical procedures which thank God helped a lot, because after short massages the paralysis subsided.

December 1, 1940

On November 28, 1940 I formally married Lizka Sokolowska. This is how it happened: I kept asking her to stay with us in Suprasl but she didn't want to and couldn't stay, because she worked at [a factory] and quitting the job without permission, missing one day of work or being a couple of minutes late was punished. As always, I came to Bialystok for the anniversary of the October Revolution, to spend a few off-work days there and suddenly this wild but also dear thought crossed my mind: "I will marry Lizeczka" and as it is with me, what I think - I do. The same day I went to the registry office and formally married my dear Lizeczka.

When I returned to Suprasl and told my mommy about it she started crying and shouting that she does not agree because I got married without her blessing and knowledge. After long and beautiful speeches, I managed to convince her that my actions were right and she accepted the fact. When Liza came to us after all that, mommy hugged and kissed her and said, crying: "Why didn't you ask me for my blessing?" We will have a ritual marriage, if God allows, when my dear daddy comes back and both mommy and Lizka agree. I feel good as a young husband, although Lizka still lives in Bialystok.

January 27, 1941

We are still in Suprasl and wait for the end of war and our liberation… I have a good job now as the chief stoker responsible for supplying fuel for all the factories. There is quite a lot of work but it is interesting and dynamic which means that I have to run around all day long to check if the factories have enough fuel…I do my best in this new job and it allows me to forget and keeps me happy…

The political news is not favorable. Germans mock England. London and other larger English cities are bombed constantly. England's response is very weak. All Europe now is under the control or influence of the "Axis powers."… Dear daddy is finally going to China [Shanghai]. We got the message via telegraph and after that we ordered a telephone call with Kaunas, because we have also thought about leaving. Unfortunately it didn't work out because the line was damaged. After a pointless attempt to talk, with our throats sore from constantly shouting "Hello", at 2 a.m. we went home. Happy travels my dear father and may God allow us to meet as soon as possible and stay together forever. It's such a pity that I could not hear your beloved voice before you left. Goodbye daddy. Stay in good health and maybe we will see each other after the war!

February 12, 1941

This is Lizka's birthday but because we had a big argument we will not spend this birthday together, she will be in B-stock

and I will be in Suprasl. So boring. There is nowhere to go.....
How come such an empire as England allows the Germans to
do what they want in Europe? Doesn't Russia see that after
the Balkans and England it will be there turn? Idiots, or is
there a game played here that only a few people running the
governments know about? But we will see - if we live that
long - how this will all turn out.

March 5, 1941

Nothing new, only boredom and searching for some
entertainment which is completely gone. I flirt with Basia
H. with great enthusiasm. I am only embarrassed by the
fact that I am cheating on Lizka but she is not here and she
deserves this a bit for the headaches she caused me with her
actions regarding our room.

March 15, 1941

Recently we got a second letter from daddy. The previous
one came from Moscow, this one from the Russian-Chinese
border from the quarantine zone. He writes that in two weeks
he will be in China, in Shanghai. He only needs to go through
a compulsory two week quarantine. This letter helped us
very much in saving mommy because it significantly lifted
her spirit.

May 25, 1941

I was in Bialystok and "stepped on the gas." I met Lizka
[and friends] and we went to "Lux" for 100 grams which
ended with 2 liters of vodka. I got seriously drunk, so
much in fact that I don't remember how I got out of the
bar. I lost consciousness and I don't remember what I did
that night. From what Lizka told me, I made "quite some

noise", and only thanks to Finka I didn't go to the "joint" [jail] *for ten years for hooliganism and counterrevolution. Supposedly I shouted unimaginable things, like: "Down with communism!, Long live democracy!" etc. They tell me that I alternated between laughing and crying and when I met Soviet soldiers I wanted to fight them and my friends barely managed to pull me away.*

I have to give one to the Soviets, B-stok now looks much prettier than during the Polish times. The Soviet government tries their best to turn B-stok into a big city. There are almost no small shops left. Two or three small shops were turned into huge stores with 4-5 display windows. They like the American-style stores where you can get every type of food product. Of course hardly anyone makes use of these things because the prices compared to salaries are impossible, even laughably high....At night the army is constantly marching towards the border, there are rumors of huge maneuvers in the border area.

June 22, 1941

Soviet-German War! God only knows! Keep us in Your Mercy! This event of historic significance in the course of humanity hit us like lightning from a clear sky. Nobody expected it. There were of course rumors of an upcoming war but not so soon and so unexpected. Everything played in front of me as if in a cinema....At 4 a.m. we were woken up by the sound of airplane engines and salvos of anti-aircraft cannons and machine gun fire. We all cursed the Soviet organization, saying "even on a Sunday they won't let you sleep."

At this point one of the neighbors came rushing into our apartment shouting, "This is war! These are German planes!" Hearing that I sprung to my feet and wearing only socks and bathing shorts, I ran to the balcony. The view was worth watching. In the clear azure sky, in the fresh, cold summer air, the black planes were circling like vultures; each had three engines and one could easily discern the black cross on a yellow backdrop on the wings.

They were surrounded by rings of smoke from the exploding Soviet anti-aircraft artillery, red streaks of shrapnel and tracer rounds from machine-guns. I stood there enchanted, gazing into the beautiful and at the same time dangerous view. I noticed that the air trembled with explosions and a plume of smoke and dirt rose from the street...

The house shook to its foundations and in the distance I could hear the sound of breaking glass. This broke my idleness and I rushed back into the room, ordering everyone to get dressed. That very same moment I heard a terrible noise combined with a rain of rubble and pieces of shattered glass. All doors were pulled from their hinges....The air became stuffy. We couldn't breathe. In the distance I could hear people crying for help. When the rain of shrapnel stopped I went out of the room and realized that one of the bombs hit our house but fortunately it went ricochet....The radio is silent. What will happen next? I don't know myself if I would like the Soviets or Germans to win. I don't like the former and detest the latter.

June 27, 1941

Soviets are retreating. They are getting beaten to a pulp. The red armies are fleeing east day and night. There is a glow over B-stock. The military magazines are burning. It is impossible to understand that after so much time spent on preparing for war, with such a great number of mechanical weapons, the Soviets are beaten so badly....German aviation

25

is constantly bombing cities and the frantically retreating Red Army. The authorities are long gone leaving the town to its own fate.

All the warehouses which the Soviets did not manage to empty or burn down have been plundered by civilians... We are expecting Germans any day now. The tension this is causing is terrifying, especially for us the Jewish population. You can't buy anything and there is nothing to eat...Money is now completely worthless...We spend our days listening to the radio but we cannot learn anything certain because Soviets and Germans broadcast only propaganda and the English radio is hard to understand because the Germans jam it.... The common suspicion is that the Germans will soon win this war...They move forward very rapidly. What will happen when they come for us? What of the Jews?

June 28, 1941

German have taken B-stok and Suprasl....Armored cars, preceded by motorcycles and light tanks drove in like specters. A few hours later came the motorized infantry in trucks. All of them are tall, square-shouldered men, armed to the teeth, suspiciously eyeing every civilian... The factories are being nationalized and put at the disposal of the German government.

On the very first day they introduced a system of compulsory work...

B-stok is terribly destroyed.

We [the Jewish police] *were leading captured artillery horses as we walked through the entire city. A terrible scene. The main streets disfigured and the most beautiful ones no longer existing, huge piles of rubble, skeletons of burnt-out houses. The Great Synagogue has disappeared from the face of the earth. This district was set on fire out of spite by the Germans and the rowdy Prussian soldiers threw living people in to the fire which burned for six days. There was such bestiality, for example they caught a father and son, the father had to throw his son into the fire and only then was thrown after him. I shook like in a fever when I walked through the streets. I couldn't get to Lizka despite making several attempts.*

July 21, 1941

They took our radios. No matter - Poles and Jews alike - the only ones allowed to keep them were Germans. Germans are certain of their victory and say they will be in Moscow in two weeks at most and the war will end with their victory... Recently they have introduced so-called "yellow patches" for Jews... This is supposed to be a sign of disgrace! I personally do not see anything disgraceful in this, should the fact that I am a Jew be a disgrace? Did I kill someone or steal something? Recently all those suspected of communism have been shot without a trial. They shot some 25 people. They also shot the Rabbi of Suprasl. That's a communist for you?

These executions were preceded by roundups and raids of so-called "partisans", but in fact they went from door to door, took all the men of Jewish faith and ran them to Bialystok's prisoner camp, beating them on the way. If anyone was not able to keep up with the pace he was shot on the spot...

When Germans came to my house and asked who lives here Jews or Poles? I answered "Pole" and this saved me... German soldiers pillage, rape and murder people every day.

Gestapo and the German police are particularly diligent in this....The nervous tension lately has been terrible.

August 17, 1941

The smear campaign against Jews is terrible. They beat us not only physically but also morally. They abuse us at every step, persecute us everywhere. Thanks to the Germans it seems that I have become more of a communist. I pray to God for the return of Russian rule. Back then I could at least be sure of the next day, now I am not even sure of the next hour....

In Bialystok they have created a ghetto for Jews...I was in B-stok on the last day before the closing of the ghetto's gates. The sight was terrible. Thousands of people kicked and beaten, with meager packs on their backs running down the city streets. Jews everywhere were beaten by Germans and Poles incited by the Germans without a sign of mercy - every person they encountered no matter if it was a man, woman or child. There were even cases of murders. The murderers show their power on the defenseless.

August 21, 1941

I will keep this day in my memory for the rest of my life. On the [previous] evening announcements were posted that all the Jews of Suprasl are supposed to appear the next day at 9 a.m. sharp in the city square with their families and children. The panic was horrifying. We were expecting the worst.

The next morning all the Jews were in the square ready to depart. Everyone was wearing 2-3 sets of clothing, had a few sets of underwear and a small package of food....Attendance was checked, official greetings made and we stood there as if on burning coals, uncertain of our fate. Poles and Germans stood all around us, looking at us as if we were some foreign animals. [But after a few hours they all were sent home and] many robbers and anti-Semites were very disappointed because all the Jewish property, which they assumed was already theirs, had to be returned to their rightful owners. Thank God it ended with just a scare.

Within the next year the Nazis liquidated all Jewish communities in the province. Some fled to join the partisans but more than 40,000 remained in the ghetto and for awhile David and his mother remained in Suprasl.

September 3, 1941

Aunt Fryda was recently in the ghetto in Bialystok and told me that it's not bad over there. Everyone leaves the ghetto to go to work and when they are in the city they buy and sell various things. At first when the Germans had just come, some idiots greeted them with flowers, saying, "They will rebuild Poland for us!" And the tiger will live in one house with a sheep - good thinking people.

January 7, 1942

One more year has passed like a bad dream. One more year of being uncertain of my life. What's next? Nothing new in politics. The Germans got all the way to Moscow and sit there immobile. Englishmen are asleep, they wage war with Germans but only using words. The end is nowhere to be seen...We sell or exchange our personal belongings for food. Everyone gets paid but the Jews.

February 12, 1942

Hurray! America has joined the war on the coalition side. At the same time Japan declared war on the U.S.A. and they have landed their troops in the Philippines...There are currently huge naval battles in the Pacific Ocean between American, British and Dutch fleets and the Japanese Navy. So far the luck has been on Japan's side...We are almost constantly on the "warpath" with our Judenrat, because paid protection and bribery are flourishing beautifully...there is no way of dealing with the German government so you have to do what they say until you are ready to burst.

March 3, 1942

Terrible rumors have reached us recently which turned out to be true, namely: the slaughtering of 10,000 Jews in Slonim [about 150 km away.] It supposedly happened in three stages, the murderers must have rested during such a hard and responsible task. There are rumors of pogroms in Vilnius and these will likely turn out true...Recently I got a good new job as a draftsman and on the occasion we drank some "moonshine" and spent the evening quite well.

June 12, 1942

Recently there has been a new rumor, so horrible and outlandish that I can't believe it. They say that in Treblinka the Germans have built a "death factory."

That is where they send Jews and other "enemies of the German nation." They are killed there with gas and their bodies burned to ashes which are then spread over fields as artificial fertilizer. The first batches of human material have supposedly already been sent there.

August 1, 1942

I recently visited Lizka in Bialystok where I got a lot of news, namely that B-stock was bombed at night by Soviet airplanes. One of the bombs landed in the ghetto and killed 20 people. When I was at Lizka's house playing cards the roof caved in and we survived only by a miracle.

October 27, 1942

Finally I can return to writing after such a long break. The most recent blow that fate has struck me was horrible! It struck me like lightning from a clear sky. Only by some miracle I managed to keep more or less composed. On the night of 15ᵗʰ September at 3 a.m. my beloved Mommy has died, She died like a saint on the eve of the Jewish New Year, She had an easy death because she died of a heart attack in her sleep....The next day, upon hearing the news of Mommy's death, Lizka came to Suprasl. She cried with me, trying to comfort me in my inconsolable grief. When Mother was still at home, it all seemed relatively fine but when I returned from the funeral, the apartment seemed empty....

After the funeral and sitting through a week of atonement, I went to the synagogue every day where I said kaddish and decided that I will mourn and wear black for the entire year....The Germans conduct searches every day, robbing, beating and breaking whatever they can. They comfort us by saying that we shouldn't worry because we will soon go to Treblinka anyway. Treblinka is now a certain and proven fact. The Warsaw Jews are right now being transported to the place of execution.

The Germans ordered the *Judenrat* to set up a police force and David was one of about 200 young men who were conscripted. Some were corrupt and took bribes, but most were members of the intelligentsia or the relatively well-off middle-class who merely were seeking an opportunity for relative safety.

November 15, 1942

> *I had to circle this date in black. Misfortunes rain over me as if from a horn of plenty. Private and general Jewish misfortunes alike....On November 1 1941 they started to deport Jews from the entire former Bialystok province and only by a miracle I managed to escape this whole affair....As I have already written, just after mom died I was thinking of moving to Bialystok to join the Jewish Security Service Corps. This was successful and I moved my belongings from Suprasl to Bialystok and became a "Jewish policeman" in the ghetto...*
>
> *We heard rumors of Jews being evacuated to Treblinka in order to make "soap." I was supposed to go but following my intuition, and fate, I remained in Bialystok...The work in the police service is quite interesting, however every policeman or commander, bah, even the commandant himself, can be bought for one kilogram of butter.*

December 1, 1942

> *When will this war finally end? The second winter is already coming and the end is nowhere to be seen. I don't like working as a policeman anymore, the work is quite hard and on top of that contemptible. There are no earnings. I live from selling my belongings... There are constant rumors about a pogrom and deportation of Bialystok Jews to Treblinka....At Stalingrad Germans got their arses kicked and are retreating.*

December 24, 1942

The days flow monotonously, like beads of a rosary. We sit here like mice in a trap, awaiting the end. A new development every hour. Old women's news claims that quite soon we will be shipped to Treblinka. I personally will not lose hope until the last moment. I have a deep-rooted feeling that I will live through this war somehow....

I believe in my star and God's protection, whom my dear momma asks to save me. Our ghetto has been reduced to 3,000 people who instead of going to Treblinka were moved to new apartments.....I made the decision! I married my Lizeczka on December 16. Now she is my official religious wife. All of our relatives were at the wedding and later, accompanied by my closest friends, we went to my place for a "schnapps." The evening was pleasant but it cost me a lot...I don't regret it because there is no saying what tomorrow will bring.

The rumors of Treblinka do not go away and appear in new forms each time. The Jews are being murdered in the following way: The people are stripped naked and walked into a huge bathhouse which is sealed behind them, and they suffocate because of heat and lack of air. Their bodies are burned, and the ashes are used for fertilizing fields. This is abhorrent and disgusting. I don't want to think about it. I'd rather die from a bullet here than in the beastly way over there....Next year is approaching and with it new hopes for the future. For life or death. It's time for this war to end! Enough of this slaughter of nations! Down with the war!

January 3, 1943

It is already 1943 but the year has begun very badly because on New Year's Eve the Germans hanged three people in the ghetto. Our new ruler, Stormfuehrer Dybus, is an exceptional bastard. Sadist and a terrible anti-Semite…[When the Gestapo commander] *visits the ghetto, it looks like a ghost town because he issued an order that he does not want to see even a single Jew on the streets and, to that end, we* [the police] *chase all the people from the streets and gather them in courtyards.*

One day he discovered three Jews coming back to the ghetto from work carrying several kilos of sunflower seeds which he believed to be stolen. For that he hanged them in front of the Judenrat, as he said, as a "scare", so that people didn't steal! It made a terrible impression on me. It is the first execution in my life which I had to assist with. This criminal put nooses on their necks himself, and he did it with such joy and a smile on his face, that it seemed like some normal everyday activity. May the Bolsheviks come and free us from these hyenas in human skins.

February 3, 1943

Thanks to the protection of my good friend Lolek Goldberg….I got the "Gate" and I think I will manage to earn some money. I have good partners….and one shmuck…so I think we can have a schnapps. The mood in the ghetto is terrible. Pogrom is now predicted every day….Supposedly, according to the Poles, they have prepared wagons for Jews for February 6. The whole city is going mad. Everyone looks for a place to hide but nobody knows where. There is panic among the officials. Judenrat is not working…..There is something evil hanging in the air. Calm before a storm. I don't know what it is, but inside I'm very agitated. My friends hope that nothing will happen. I also say that...Let's hope it will be fine.

February 5, 1943

The aktion has begun! The manhunt started at 4 a.m.! The rumors turned out to be true. This day which I have survived is one bad dream. It seems impossible that I could live through something like this...I stood with my friends, it was like a torture. Grown men were weeping like children and biting their fingers and lips in silent despair, drawing blood. People were running back and forth like mad. Of course we [the Jewish police] made a lot of noise and let through everyone who tried to escape the dangerous streets while not letting anyone in. The night was dark and gloomy. It was raining a bit, there was barely any air to breathe.

At 4 a.m. sharp we heard a gunshot...the horrible tragedy has begun. I didn't know what was happening around me. In my soul I prayed to God for mercy if not on me, then at least on my closest relatives. We stood there until 4:30 a.m. The darkness faded into ghastly paleness of a misty dawn. It was so silent that I could hear the beating of my own heart. In the distance we could hear gunshots.

We were told that the Commander wanted to see us. We were met by this bandit, in company of his Gestapo officers, and upon seeing us they attacked like rabid dogs, beating us and shouting that we have betrayed them because there are no people in the apartments...While beating us with batons and rifle butts they made us stand in the middle of the street and pointed their guns at us....[We were told] that if within the next 1/2 hour we will not find 500 people we will be shot! I knew at once we will not find 50 people so I was ready to die....They ordered us to walk from door to door and drag people out. We were supposed to be their hunting dogs. All this time I only asked for a quick death, to be shot directly in the head

Suddenly there were explosions and bullets flying. Amidst the chaos, David and other members of the Jewish police ran away and hid in a closet for an entire day, afraid to move and holding their breath.

We could hear screams of people being murdered in the adjacent yards, pleased German shouts, gunshots and sounds of doors being broken down. All the time I prayed to God to allow me to survive this and see my daddy again. 100 people were shot and in general, they were shooting everyone in sight. At 11 p.m. I went to see what is happening. The city looked deserted, there were dead bodies everywhere. Old men with crushed heads, women with their intestines ripped out with bayonets and men shot to death. The parcels belonging to the people were lying in the streets. What will happen next?

February 6, 1943

The aktion was underway. The sounds of gunshots and doors being broken down were coming from every direction... Armed with crowbars, axes and shovels, we marched [and I was sent to Gate III.] There was a German awaiting us who - having requisitioned a Polish wagon - ordered us to load it with bodies of dead Jews who jumped from the train or the ghetto wall. We gathered six bodies this way. It's strange how good is these murderers' aim. Almost all of the dead have been shot in the head. The wounds are terrible. Whole parts of the head simply torn away by the bullet... The dead are deposited next to the mortuary because there is no more room inside. There are more than 600 dead bodies from yesterday. This day will bring at least as many more....

Today I took a night shift so that tomorrow I don't have to take part in the "hunt." The night was peaceful. I went to sleep at 7 a.m.

February 8, 1943

The hunt began anew....I took a wagon to gather the bodies. I prefer to deal with the dead than the living. At least I don't do them any harm by my work. The sight of the cemetery is terrifying, literally heaps of dead bodies lying on top of each other. Bodies mangled by grenades, strangled children and dead people looking at the sky with their misty eyes. God make the Soviets come as soon as possible. There would be no better communist than me in the whole wide world. I pray that B-stok gets bombed. A Rabbi wisely said: "Jews! Put on your mourning clothes and sprinkle ash on your head because God is dead!"

February 10, 1943

The hunt for people started as usual at 7 a.m. My nerves are on the very brink of failing. I felt as if I was electrified....A new sect has appeared in the ghetto as a result of the "action," the so-called "mosers" [traitors.] These were people who when they were found and sent to the transport, betrayed others in order to save their own lives....I remain alive and sane.

February 13, 1943

The aktion is over....I realized how tired I was. I could barely stand straight and went home where I slept for 30 hours straight. When I woke up, with a friend I went out into the street full of people. I saw a disgusting scene. Two men were pulling shoes off the feet of some forgotten corpse which was calmly lying there…There is the following news regarding the casualties of the "action": 12,000 people evacuated for "soap" to Treblinka so we must consider the possibility of their death….

Only individuals who jumped off the trains might have saved themselves. 1,800 were killed by Germans on the spot or died of hunger in shelters. 14,800 people in total [killed or wounded]…For a "man-hunt" that lasted only a week the results are very good. The Germans will have something to boast about after the war - which they will surely lose…I would like these damned Prussians and Krauts to feel such an "action" on their own skin.

February 27, 1943

Of course we [the Jewish police] did this work very reluctantly. I was ashamed to look in people's eyes when walking around in my police cap - a cap dripping with blood, a cap which turned me into a traitor of the Jewish nation and forced me to help the Germans murder innocent people - but I had to wear it, and I still have to, because this bloodied cap is my shelter, my life's safeguard. If I'm not to think of myself, then my damn duty is to at least protect my closest family Maybe if they fired me that would be different but I will never have the guts to do it myself. They are now talking about reducing the [police] corps. If they fire me - fine, if not - fine as well. May fate lead me. I cannot do anything now and cannot make any decision.

March 8, 1943

The same aktion as in B-stock is currently taking place in Warsaw. But the Warsaw Jews stood up much nicer than the ones in Bialystok. They have entered an alliance with the Home Army and are meeting the Germans with armed resistance. The fight is still continuing, the Warsaw Ghetto is under siege. Glory to the heroic Jews of Warsaw!

March 15, 1943

The gate [job] is going well...I made acquaintances with the Germans, two of them in particular. One of them is a Berliner, chauffeur and communist, who was forced to wear the German gendarme uniform. Before leaving for holiday he shook my hand and told unbelievable things about the fuehrer. The second one is a Saxonian, a very intelligent guy, with a great knowledge of politics. Often when we are posted together we discuss political matters. His opinions are the same as mine...he says that the Germans have lost the war. He thinks that after the war they will treat Germans the same way the Germans are treating Jews now....May God allow us to avenge ourselves and take up arms against the Germans - this plague who periodically strive to destroy the world.

April 21, 1943

The ghetto is calm right now, I hope it stays this way. New spies appeared among us cooperating with the Gestapo. They walk without the patches and are allowed to leave the ghetto...I hope Hitler chokes on as many murders as the number of people they brought to misery...

It is the fourth [Passover] holiday that I celebrate alone or with strangers... Well what can you do? It's war... I'm now in charge of traffic. The work is not good and I have to constantly argue with people. I would like to quit the Z.S.P. [Jewish police.]

May 28, 1943

> *The Warsaw Jews defending the ghetto against the Germans*
> *have been finally defeated and are now buried under the*
> *rubble of the houses they had turned into strongholds. Anti-*
> *German movements have appeared in Bialystok and the*
> *region.*

July 12, 1943

> *I have gotten very sick…my nerves are at their very limit. For*
> *some time I have entertained thoughts of suicide but thanks*
> *to Lizka and uncle Szmul I managed somehow to stay alive.*
> *On July 3 I received a letter from my one and only daddy, my*
> *only anchor. My only dream is to survive and see him again.*
> *The letter was brought by a Jew working at the post office…*
> *Recently I sold my last suit.*

That was the last legible entry in David Spiro's diary. According to historian Tomek Wisniewski, it was written at a time when German and Ukrainian soldiers were shooting people in Bialystok's streets "just for fun." Perhaps David was one of them.

During the roughly two year Soviet period in Bialystok, intellectuals, capitalists and anyone considered to be untrustworthy "enemies of the people" were deported to Siberian gulags. As factory owners David's father and several relatives recognized the danger and fled to the East. A few of David's relatives survived the war and although today their descendants are scattered throughout the world, none seem to have been aware of the existence of David Spiro or of his diary. What might have become of this young man if he'd survived the Holocaust? Perhaps he might have been among those who were eager to forget, if not forgive, and withdrawn into silence. Or perhaps he would have become an activist crying "Never again.

5

Archives

In the Warsaw Ghetto historian Emanuel Ringelblum felt a need to write "from inside the event" and encouraged witnesses to record their impressions immediately so they wouldn't be skewed by the distorting lens of selective memory. It was vital to capture the everyday details of Jewish life under German occupation in order to meld individual testimonies into a collective portrait. As Ringlelblum explained, "These documents and notes are a remnant resembling a clue in a detective story...We are noting the evidence of a crime."

In Bialystok the young resistance leader Mordecai Tenenbaum knew of Ringelblum's project and similarly felt compelled to preserve documents as a testimony for future generations. Assisted by Tzvi Mersik he began collecting materials that reflected everyday life in the ghetto. Not as well known today as the archive assembled in Warsaw, what now is called the Mersik-Tenenbaum Underground Archive since 1955 has been stored at Yad Vashem in Jerusalem with some materials and/or copies also owned by the Ghetto Fighters' House in the Western Galilee and by the Jewish Historical Institute in Warsaw. 2

Tzvi Mersik began interviewing survivors from nearby towns and after he contracted a fatal case of typhoid fever, Tenenbaum and several others continued the project. Most of the documents were written in Yiddish and included minutes of *Judenrat* meetings, posters, poems and personal testimonies. Once after reading scraps of writing found in discarded clothing of two individuals who'd perished at Treblinka, Tenenbaum wrote, "I wade through them all day and cannot stop for a minute. It feels as if my pockets are on fire. It's monstrous appalling."

After several months of gathering documents, Tenenbaum placed the archive in sealed tin boxes and aluminum milk cans that were buried outside the ghetto by a sympathetic Pole. After the war, it took more than a year before a map was discovered that helped locate them - although there may have been a third box it was never found.

Mordecai Tenenbaum's diary was written in Hebrew and although no complete English translation exists, substantial portions can be read in the translation of Sarah Bender's book (cited earlier.) To Mordecai the main function of the resistance was to defend the honor of the Jewish people. In a letter to Zionist leaders in Palestine: "With these lines I want to establish a memorial, however inadequate, for those dearest to me who are no longer with us. Comrades, the movement feels honored to have produced such people, people who have spent months preparing for a beautiful death. Can there be such a thing? Do not forget them."

In an epilogue to her memoir, survivor Chaika Grossman wrote that more than once Mordecai had read to her what he'd written before it was sent to be hidden outside the ghetto"

> *I knew that [his] words were written in moments of tension, when the writer wavered between hope and despair over the future of the ghetto, the people, political leaders, institutions, movements, and the Judenrat. They were penned in fragments, hurriedly, feverishly, almost automatically, without any real opportunity to balance, analyze or summarize. That is perhaps the great historic value of Mordecai Tenenbaum's entries.* (C. Grossman, p. 398)

On January 13, 1943 Tenenbaum reported, "I wrote a manifesto calling for a stand and defense. This is the third manifesto that I have written - the first was in Warsaw, the second in Grodno and the third here in Bialystok." (S. Bender, p. 350, note 46.) Written in

Yiddish, this document exhorted the ghetto's desperate youth to resist but it wasn't distributed for six months until "the moment when we proclaim the counteraction." Then, just before the start of the final liquidation and uprising, Daniel Moskowicz, the second in command to Mordecai, instructed women of the underground to distribute handbills of the manifesto throughout the ghetto:

Fellow Jews. Fearsome days have come upon us. More than the ghetto and the yellow badge, hatred, humiliation and degradation - we now face death! Before our own eyes our wives and children, fathers and mothers, brothers and sisters are being led to the slaughter. Thousands have already gone; tens of thousands will shortly follow. In these terrible hours, as we hover between life and death, we appeal to you.

Be aware - five million European Jews have already been murdered in Europe by Hitler and his henchmen. All that remains of Polish Jewry is about ten percent of the original Jewish community. In Chelmo and in Belzec, in Auschwitz and in Treblinka, in Sobibor and in other camps more than three million Polish Jews were tortured and butchered. Don't kid yourselves - all transports lead to death!

Do not believe the Gestapo propaganda about letters supposedly received from the evacuees. That is a damnable lie! The road on which the deportees have gone leads to gigantic crematoria and mass graves in the thicket of the Polish forests. Each one of us is condemned. You have nothing to lose! Work can no longer save you.

After the first liquidation there will be a second and a third - until the last Jew is killed. Dividing the ghetto into various categories is a sophisticated Gestapo method of deceiving us and making their dirty work easier. Jews, we are being led to Treblinka! Like leprous beasts we will be gassed and cremated. Let us not passively go like sheep to the slaughter. Even though we are too weak to defend our lives, still we are strong enough to preserve our Jewish honor and human dignity and to show the world that although they have broken our bodies, they have not broken our spirits! We have not yet fallen.

Do not go willingly to your death. Fight for your lives until your last breath! Attack your executioners with tooth and nail, with axes and knives, with acid and iron rods. If we fall as heroes, even in our death…we shall not die. Let the enemy pay for blood with blood. Their death for our death! Will you cower in your corners when your nearest and dearest are humiliated and put to death?

Will you sell your wives and children, your parents, your soul for another few weeks of slavery? Let us ambush the enemy, kill and disarm him, wage resistance against the murderers. And if necessary - die like heroes. Except for our honor we have nothing to lose! Do not sell your lives cheaply!

Avenge the destroyed communities and uprooted settlements. When you leave your homes, set fire to them. Burn and demolish the factories. Do not let the hangman inherit our possessions! Jewish youth! Follow the example of generations of Jewish fighters and martyrs, dreamers and builders, pioneers and activists - go out and fight.

Hitler will lose the war. Slavery and murder will vanish from the face of the earth. The world will one day be cleansed and purified….For the sake of mankind's bright future you must not die like dirty dogs! To the forest, to the resistance fighters. Do not flee the ghetto unarmed, for without weapons you will perish. Only after fulfilling your national obligation, go to

*the forest armed. Weapons can be seized from any German
in the ghetto. BE STRONG!*
(B. Klibanski, *Yad Vashem Studies* 2(1958) 328-9; S. Bender,
p. 256. Reprinted with permission of Brandeis University
Press.)

It's remarkable that Mordecai Tenenbaum's manifesto is virtually unknown today. To be sure, similar manifestos exhorting armed resistance were distributed in the Warsaw and Vilna ghettos and it's astonishing to realize that nearly every detail of what befell European Jewry became known to Jews trapped in Bialystok's ghetto while the world waited and watched. **3**

Another Bialystok diarist **Pesach Kaplan** had edited a daily newspaper (*Unzer Lebn*) before the war and now was a member of the *Judenrat*. He'd also been a social activist, book translator and musicologist and in the ghetto he organized a school system. Kaplan's diary began "How does one describe the destruction of Bialystok as the author of the Book of Lamentations would have adequately done? It is possible for me only to record cut and dry facts indelibly inscribed in my memory about the recent bleak and bloody days." Immediately after the Germans returned in June 1941, Pesach Kaplan described the mood:

> *Our souls are tortured by the unanswerable question: how
> much longer will our lives be prolonged — for days or for
> weeks? Optimists believe we will be permitted to live for
> another month while the pessimists disagree. People move
> about like shadows, physically and mentally shattered, their
> gazes reflecting hope extinguished, moving automatically
> through inertia, like lunatics.* (S. Bender, p. 98. Reproduced
> by permission of Brandeis University Press.)

The wives of those who were taken away on Saturday July 3 were known as Sabbath widows (*di shabbesdike*) and Pesach Kaplan's poem expressed their anguish:

Rivkele the Sabbath widow
works in the factory
spins threads
twines cord
Oh the ghetto's so dark
It's been too long already
Her heart contracts
with too much pain
Her darling Hershel
has gone, departed.
Since that Sabbath
that moment
Rivkele mourns
Day and night she weeps
and besides the loom
sits and ponders
Where is my beloved?
Perhaps he's alive? Where?
Perhaps in a concentration camp
Working his knuckles to the bone?
It's so hard for him there
So hard for her here
Since that Sabbath
that moment.
(S. Bender. Reproduced by permission of Brandeis University Press.)

Pesach Kaplan continued to record daily events until March 1943 when he contracted a fatal infection. His last entry: "Remember when the time comes for taking revenge, pay them back for what they have done."

6

Aktions

The first of the final two major aktions began on February 5, 1943 and later became known as "the February Action." Each morning at dawn soldiers entered the ghetto, rounded up Jews and took them away to the transports. At night residents in hiding prepared for the next day's onslaught and when the round-up came to an end after about a week, Mordecai Tenenbaum described the scene as survivors emerged from their shelters:

> Only now one begins to comprehend the full gruesomeness of the past few days; scores of crazed people are running through town looking for their kin. They run and fall, get up and fall again. Smothered children are being dragged from the shelters. They began crying during the searches and were suffocated. It seems everyone is carrying belongings. Everywhere there are tears…At the cemetery, gigantic heaps of dead bodies are buried in mass graves. Again, loud wailing. "Today snow has fallen, covering the bloodstains on the ground. Underneath the whiteness of the snow appears a shiny redness. In the afternoon it rained. All has been washed away.

Two weeks after the February aktion, Mordecai told the remaining Jews: "We are surrounded by the dead. We know what took place in Warsaw. No one was left alive….We are the last to survive. It is not a particularly comfortable feeling to be the last. It is a special responsibility.

Now is the time to decide how to act tomorrow." But then there was a six month interval of relative calm and the *Judenrat* urged people to work, pay taxes and bills, and keep their apartments and yards clean. When the first news of what was happening at Treblinka came in March, Tenenbaum wrote "There are no more illusions....our only option is defense."

The final liquidation began on August 15, 1943 when German and Ukrainian troops surrounded the ghetto in three tight rings. The *Judenrat* was caught off guard by the Nazis who fostered a false sense of security by saying that the entire population would be relocated to Lublin. By then the young activists had accumulated a hundred pistols, a dozen rifles and one machine gun that either were smuggled in or produced in hidden workshops.

The next day Tenenbaum and more than 100 young comrades launched the final revolt, mostly by throwing home-made grenades and Molotov cocktails. But the Germans had learned from experience recently gained in the Warsaw Ghetto uprising and were well prepared. To over 3,000 heavily armed SS troops they added armored vehicles, tanks and aircraft. The battle raged for five days but unable to break out of the ghetto, about 70 fighters retreated into a bunker where all were shot. It's believed that as the last resistance positions fell, Mordecai Tenenbaum saved the last bullet for himself.

7

First Responders

After the city was liberated by the Red Army several Bialystokers returned and among them was **Yisroel (Srolke) Kot** who'd escaped to join the partisans in the forests. As he approached the city, he saw peasants in the fields gathering hay. Others stood chatting in front of their homes as if nothing had happened:

> *I was happy that I would see [Bialystok] again, but I was filled with pain and gnawing doubts about what I would find. Logic and the information available to me dictated that I would come upon desolation, but my heart said otherwise. Maybe I would find someone, a loved one or a friend. Coming to the outskirts of town, I saw chimney stacks that had been torn from destroyed houses, blown up bridges, the railroad station gutted. Whole streets lay empty before me; other streets had entirely disappeared....It was hard to believe anyone had ever lived here.*
>
> *Then I walked toward what had been my home. I had left it the year before, without my brother and sister. The cobblestone pavement leading to the house was almost completely covered with grass, a sign that people had not walked there in many months. It was as if the stones cried out in anguish: the grass cannot cover us! Generations of*

Jews had made a life for themselves here and we must tell their saga!

Homes were demolished, walls absent, windows and doors missing. Jewish books were strewn everywhere. Furniture was damaged - chairs without legs, dressers without drawers, broken beds, feathers from torn mattresses…Photographs of the people who had once lived in these houses: men with beards and sidelocks or with heads uncovered, women with their traditional wigs or sporting the latest hairdos… Surely all this could not have been wiped off the face of the earth. The victims' spilled blood cried out: What did they do to us and why?

I approached my house slowly, as if I were being led to execution…not even the shell remained intact, denying me the opportunity of getting down on my knees, having a good cry, holding on to a wall like a child who, having fallen, seeks to get back on his feet by supporting himself against something stable.

All I found were some broken foundation stones and half a chimney. Looking about I tried to pinpoint where the window and the door had been. Where was the bed in which I had slept? It was horrible to imagine that no one knew anything about the thousands of Jews who might have survived, who had populated Bialystok only a year before. Only a few returned, some entering this building to spend the night after rummaging through the streets for a few morsels of food.

Standing on top of my home's ruin, I could not help but recall the tragedy that had befallen my family and the rest of the Jewish people. Why did they have to suffer such brutality needlessly, except for the fact they were Jews? The air I breathed was filled with the smoke of the crematories of

Treblinka, Majdanek, Auschwitz and other death camps....
At that moment, I felt utterly powerless. My feet, which had
carried me thousands of miles through forests and highways,
muddy roads and underground passageways, seeking to
escape the grim fate of my people, buckled.

My survival seemed meaningless as I spotted a portion of
the barbed wire fence, a remnant of the destroyed Bialystok
ghetto. I felt guilty that I survived and my loved ones did not.
What meaning could my life have when all the love that I
had known from childhood had been wrenched away by the
Nazis. I was torn between wanting to enter the broken frame
of my house in which, to my horror, I might find the skeletons
of my lost relatives, and leaving - which I could not physically
bring myself to do.

Nightfall arrived. I wondered how and where I would spend
the night. Walking through the wide-open streets, I searched
for other human beings, feeling marooned as if on a faraway
planet. I asked a Polish woman whether she knew any Jews.
She answered that she did not. Then, after many inquiries, I
was told that several were staying at a building on Kupiecka
Street, which I found in a state of total disrepair, making it
difficult to enter.

Those who arrived were barefoot, without any possessions.
They found a corner of the floor to sleep on. Some placed their
clenched fists underneath their heads as an uncomfortable
pillow and covered themselves with papers and books
scattered throughout the apartment. It was exceedingly
difficult to accept this reality to which we had come after
enduring years of incredible suffering.

My Jewish neighbor took me into a room with a bed, which I
hadn't seen for a whole year. She covered it with clean linen

and I went to sleep, awakening late the next day. The others
who spent the night had already left, in search of a bit more
food, hoping to survive for another day.
(S. Kot. *Bialystoker Memorial Book.* p. 121-122.)

Srolke Kot noticed a hole in the earth near a remnant of the ghetto wall and recalled that this must have been the hideout he had built for his sister and parents. He bent over and stared into the opening...How was he to deal with the fear of his own thoughts? He wondered whether this is what it meant to be liberated? (A. Zable, *Jewels and Ashes.* p. 203.)

The experience of historian **Szymon Datner**:

I became a member of the National Reconstruction Council,
which immediately plunged into the Herculean task of
rebuilding the Polish and Jewish communities in Bialystok.
In September or October 1944 it was learned that many
messages were carved in the walls of the prison in Bialystok
in Polish and Yiddish, apparently by the last remaining Jews
in the ghetto. Since these inscriptions might possess historical
significance, the reconstruction committee sent a delegation,
including me, to inspect these areas.

We found the graffiti quite legible but heart rending. As the
only Jew in the group it was my task to translate the Yiddish
words. All the inscriptions mentioned the names of their
authors, the dates on which they met their brutal deaths, and
the refrain, "Do not forget us. Avenge our death!" In death
chamber 81 three wall inscriptions were carved: "Their fate
should be worse than what they did to us Jews. The last
day of our life, July 15, 1944." These macabre words were
inscribed during the final days of Nazi rule...

On July 27, 1944, the first battalions of the Red Army
entered Bialystok, together with partisan forces containing

many Jews. The Nazis murdered a few remaining Jews until five minutes before the Russians arrived. The last testaments of their victims, however, remained scribbled on the walls of the prison. Years afterward, when I opened my notebook where I had written down the words of these martyrs, the cry for retribution still rang in my ears. How is it possible to avenge more than 100,000 Jews who perished in the Bialystok region? Can we ever fulfill their last wish? Perhaps the greatest retaliation is that we, their survivors, are here to tell their story.

(S. Datner, *Bialystoker Memorial Book.* p. 81-82)

Rabbi Awrom Krawets remembered the first Passover held after the war:

Passover was fast approaching. How would we provide matzah for the community?...Oddly, when Jews were not interested in material possessions they wanted to restore religious tradition. Thus we were resolved to bake our own matzos. We sent letters to Jews in the provinces around Bialystok, who were slightly better off financially than we were, requesting they contribute money to our matzah fund. They responded generously. In two weeks we got fourteen hundred kilograms of flour. Dr. Szymon Datner, Chairman of the Jewish Reconstruction Committee, found other sources of financial assistance, enabling us to begin baking the matzo.

On the day before Passover, Jews from the surrounding towns came to Bialystok to buy matzah. We supplied everyone. Dr. Datner and I led the seder services at our headquarters. Tables were beautifully decorated, featuring the traditional fish, meat and other delicious Passover foods. In addition, we were able to offer kosher wine, which we prepared ourselves. The people were

> *well satisfied. We spent a most enjoyable night. That*
> *Passover was indeed memorable because it filled us with*
> *hope after so much tragedy. We looked forward to a*
> *brighter future.*
> (A. Krawets. *Bialystoker Memorial Book*, p. 122-123.)

Bronia ("Bronka") Winicka met Mordecai Tenenbaum in January 1942. Neither were natives of Bialystok but had been sent there as emissaries of the Jewish underground. She was invited to a meeting of the clandestine Dror Zionist Youth organization but had to get from Grodno to Bialystok alone. Without any money the Aryan looking and self-confident young woman asked a German officer to buy a ticket for her at a train station. He did! Two months later she moved into a house in the city with five other young women who worked as "liason officers" to obtain critical weapons, gather intelligence and bring supplies to the partisans. She was the only one of these couriers who survived. Bronka, age 18, and Mordecai, age 26, became lovers but their relationship was doomed.

In her memoir titled *Ariadne* Bronka recalled her reaction when her suspicious Polish landlady gave the news that liquidation of the ghetto had begun.

> *During the night, the Germans encircled the ghetto with a*
> *large number of forces and have begun the aktion The Jews*
> *are firing. How come my landlady knows and I am sleeping*
> *peacefully? At this moment, my entire world crumbled. How*
> *wasn't I aware? Where were my senses? Where is my famous*
> *intuition? I can't even think.Three words are throbbing in my*
> *head and heart: "It has begun. It has begun!" In front of my*
> *landlady, I pretend to be calm and leave quickly the house -*
> *to run in the direction of the ghetto. My feet are carrying me*
> *there... there are my beloved. The whole purpose of my life.*
> *My street Mazowiecka is lengthy. It seems of no end. I hasten*
> *my steps.*

Suddenly Chaika [Grossman] is before me...How did she get here?...I do not show my surprise and do not ask questions. Keeping silent, without a word, we walk together...At last Chaika breaks the silence.They knew about the underground and the active resistant movement. Guards are positioned, all the passages are blocked, the ghetto will be destroyed... People are thunderstruck. A feeling of being trapped. They don't even try to hide. The element of surprise suppressed every will....Chaika did not once pronounce the name of Mordecai although she knew. I was dying to ask but did not. Something holds me back. I know. He will not stay alive. He will fight till the end.

Bronka ended by describing how a few Jews had a last chance to escape by jumping from the deportation trains: "Those who will try, and succeed to remain alive will reach the partisans. Not one of my comrades remained alive. They fought to the end. They are the heroes of a glorious chapter in our history." Bronka Winicka met her future husband Misha Klibanski in Bialystok. He had been a paratrooper and a partisan and in 1953 they immigrated to Israel and settled in Jerusalem. It was she who Mordecai had trusted to smuggle the archive out of the ghetto and delivered it to a member of the Polish underground and now, working at Yad Vashem, she was instrumental in preserving the previously buried documents.

Rafael Rajzner moved to Australia in 1948 and while events still were fresh in mind published a memoir in Yiddish, *The Annihilation of Bialystoker Jewry.* When he died in 1953 at age 56, a copy of the book was buried with him and some six decades later (2008) his memoir was translated to English by Dr. Henry Lew who described Rajner's eye witness account as especially important in the current era of Holocaust deniers. Rajzner had survived Auschwitz because of his printing skills, he having been assigned to a select group who were forced to make counterfeit British Pounds Sterling. Elements of his story were weaved into an Austrian film *The Counterfeiters* that was awarded the 2008 Academy Award for Best Foreign Language Film.

Henry Lew's parents were from Bialystok and the apt title of his translation of Rajzner's book was *The Stories Our Parents Found Too Painful to Tell*. Dr. Lew suggested that had it appeared a few years earlier, it might have become famous because in the first decade or so after the war people weren't yet ready to listen; they wanted to forget what had happened and return to normalcy. However, in 1960 the Anne Frank Museum opened and the next year the Eichman trial in Jerusalem generated enormous interest. Then after decades of silence, more survivors felt encouraged to tell their stories; as Henry Lew noted, "Nobody looked at Primo Levi or Elie Wiesel until the 1960s."

Chaika Grossman was born in Bialystok to relatively affluent parents, her father Nahum owned a factory in nearby Sokolka. She was the youngest of ten children, Yiddish and Hebrew were spoken at home and Polish was taught almost as a foreign language. Chaika's education began at a Hebrew school and later she attended a Polish gymnasium where she studied Marx, Freud, Schopenhauer and whatever new literature appeared in Europe between the two World Wars. At an early age she joined *Hashomer Hazair*, the Zionist & Socialist Youth Movement, her goal to become a pioneer in Israel and study at the Hebrew University. But at the end of her high school years, war was imminent and several days before the German invasion she was chosen to work in the underground movement.

Although many Jews fled in the first days of the German invasion of Soviet territory in June 1941, Chaika was fearless: "I'm not going. You men go East but not all the Jews are leaving, most are staying. I am a girl and I look Aryan. It will be easier for me." She moved relatively freely and a friend from the Polish underground supplied her with a birth certificate signed by a Catholic priest. For two years Chaika operated in various ghettos: Vilna, Warsaw, Lublin, Grodno and her home base Bialystok. She purchased and smuggled weapons and helped prepare for the Bialystok uprising. The following excerpts from Chaika Grossman's lengthy memoir *The Underground Army* describe her experience on the first day of the ghetto revolt:

It was Aug. 15, 1943, on a fine summer evening. We had gathered for a staff meeting in Mordecai's [Tenenbaum] deserted room... It was about 2 o'clock in the morning. [A courier shouted] "Get dressed. An SS unit has come in and set sentries near the factory....Now everything was clear. The liquidation had come. The morning was pale and cold, under the clear blue skies. Streets filled with Jews.... The few automatic guns in storage were distributed. Most of the girls remained unarmed, but they had a different task. The sabotage and incendiary groups were comprised mostly of girls. Others were couriers and some were nurses...(C. Grossman, p. 275-6)

Ach, Gott," we heard a cry right near us. Here the [Germans] were, hiding along the fence. We heard shooting. They were falling and groaning, not attacking us. They were frightened. "Hurrah." The whole world shook and we were reeling with the power of the guns roaring all along the fence. Suddenly we were under fire. One man lay in his blood. The house went up in flames; the adjoining houses were also burning like matchboxes....

I shot, fell, rose and ran to the fence, and then retreated with the others. I hit the barbed wire and my feet bled. I was filthy, covered with mud and soot. I shouted "hurrah" with the rest and clung to the ground with the others when the German fire grew heavier. I heard the wounded groaning, and saw a comrade fall near me. His shout was cut off....There were tanks in front of us.... A plane droned overhead. It flew low, made a number of turns and disappeared. It came back, strafing us in the fields and the streets....

Now they sent in SS infantry. We shot at them but the battlefield was narrowing. Many of them fell, but the column

*was long; they moved ahead and fired, came closer, kept
firing and the encirclement was almost complete.*

*Then the order came to try to break through the approaching
columns...Our single machine gunner was ordered to cover
the retreat. I moved and reached the house. Behind me I
heard shooting. I pressed against the wall and felt a wave of
hot air and then heard a whistle. Plaster fell at my feet. A
bullet hit the wall just a few centimeters away from me.... I
had lost my group, my comrades, and before me was only the
transport* [cattle cars to a concentration camp.]...*It was
clear: the battle was over.*

But Chaika Grossman escaped and for the next year, along with five
other young women, she arranged rescues and moved survivors to the
forests in support of the partisans. She organized an anti-Nazi group
that spied on and sabotaged German forces in Bialystok. After the war
and on the fifth anniversary of the ghetto revolt, a monument was set
up over the grave of 71 fallen rebels and on that occasion Chaika had a
powerful message:

*Five years after they fell, their remains were taken out of
the grave underneath the garbage heap...The sight of the
torn and vermin-eaten limbs brought to Jewish burial was
terrible. But no one wept over their grave. Readers, do not
weep either! But do not close your hearts and your ears. Listen
to their voices rising from the grave. See and remember, but
don't weep.* 5 (C. Grossman, pp. 290-291.)

Many years later, **Ewa Kracowska**, another fighter who survived the
ghetto and eventually settled in Israel, described her experience during
the uprising:

*On the morning of 16.8.1943, as a rank and file member,
I was positioned with two young men active in the*

*underground, at a combat spot near the Smolena street wall.
The wall was burnt but nobody was leaving as the ghetto was
already surrounded by German tanks and soldiers. At the
place where I was positioned, there were about 80 young men
and women having among them some 20 rifles and many
Molotov bottles as well as a few improvised grenades. The
Germans went into the ghetto after 9 o'clock in the morning
reaching Smolena street. I have not enough words to describe
the hell that erupted...*

*Among the Germans, I saw a number of soldiers killed and
others wounded. On the other hand, there were almost no
Jewish defenders left. The Germans captured a small number
of Jewish defenders... and parked them in the "garden" of the
Judenrat leader in order to shoot them before the eyes of
the residents who were being led to the ghetto's gate... Two
young men succeeded to take me out of the ghetto to hide
in an attic where we remained for more than two months...
The remainder of the last groups of rebels set on fire various
factories located in the Polish sector bordering the ghetto and
we saw many fires raging. To my utter sorrow, the two young
men that were with me did not survive and died later....
At present, I am probably the only one who remains alive.*
(BIALYgen. May 2003)

The Bialystok ghetto was the last to be liquidated. There were slightly
more than 40,000 Jews when the ghetto was sealed in November 1942 and
close to 30,000 when it was destroyed. In the days after the uprising, about
1,000 people were rooted out and shot; those remaining, some 7,600,
were deported: women and children to Treblinka, men to Majdanek and
Auschwitz. A train with nearly 2,000 children, accompanied by a doctor
and 53 adults, was sent to Terezin (Theresienstadt) but after six weeks
there the group was transported to Auschwitz where all were murdered
upon arrival.

The first scouts of the Red Army arrived on July 26, 1944 and early the next morning were followed by the main army who brought food, medicine and arms. The handful of Jews who were left gave a warm welcome and, in turn, the Russians organized a concert and a lecture about the international situation. Estimates vary but roughly 200 Jews from Bialystok survived the camps and several dozen survived by hiding on the Polish side of the city; 60 Jews who had joined the partisans also survived the war but before long almost all were gone.

Today, of some 300,000 residents of Bialystok, only one publicly admits to being Jewish.

8

Still More Voices

There is a letter in Mimi Sheraton's book *The Bialy People* that she received from an elderly former Bialystoker **Pesach Szmusz** who was nostalgic for the tasty morsels that originated in his hometown. In Bialystok they were called *kuchen* (cake) and had been a staple of his sparse diet. Because Szmusz was born the same year as David Spiro they might have been friends and after the war he fled to Australia in order to join his only living relative - but as he admitted later, "If I had the money I would have run right back to Poland." Pesach Szmusz ended his letter to Mimi Sheraton with this heart-breaking disclosure: "I was 20 years old in the Bialystok ghetto, 23 years old in Auschwitz and 100 years older after the liberation. I am *still* not liberated and I will not be free until my last day."

In **Samuel Pisar**'s autobiography *Of Blood and Hope* he recalled terrifying details from his childhood:

> When the ghetto liquidation in Bialystok began, only three members of our family were still alive: my mother, my little sister and I, age 13. Father had already been executed by the Gestapo. Mother told me to put on long pants, hoping I would look more like a man, capable of slave labor. "And you and Frieda?" I asked. She didn't answer. She knew that their fate was sealed.

As they were chased with the other women, the children, the old and the sick, toward the waiting cattle cars, I could not take my eyes off them. Little Frieda held my mother with one hand, and with the other, her favorite doll. They looked at me too, before disappearing from my life forever. Their train went directly to Auschwitz-Birkenau, mine to the · extermination camp of Majdanek.

Months later, I also landed in Auschwitz, still hoping naively to find their trace ... At the central ramp, surrounded by electrically charged barbed wire, we were ordered to strip naked and file past the infamous Dr. Josef Mengele. The "angel of death" performed on us his ritual "selection" – those who were to die immediately to the right, those destined to live a little longer and undergo atrocious medical experiments, to the left.
("Will We 'Never Forget'?" *Washington Post*, January 23, 2005. p. B07)

Fortunately young Samuel Pisar was sent to the left and lived to become a renowned international lawyer and honored diplomat who during his long career served as adviser to Presidents Kennedy and Nixon, Nelson Rockefeller, Henry Kissinger and Golda Meir. When he accompanied former French President Valery Giscard d'Estaing on a visit to Auschwitz in 1975, Samuel Pisar delivered a moving address:

I bear you the personal testimony of a rare survivor, perhaps the youngest survivor of all. Among the unspeakable reminiscences that flood my mind in these once-familiar surroundings, one heartbreaking image stands out...Near those machine-gun towers, in their striped blue and white rags, sat every day the most remarkable symphony orchestra ever assembled. It was made up of the greatest virtuosos from Warsaw and Paris, from Kiev and Oslo, from Budapest and Rome. The precious violins they brought along on their last journey were signed Stradivarius, Guarneri and Amati. To accompany the daily hangings and shootings - while the gas chambers over there belched fire and smoke - they were ordered to play Mozart, the Mozart that you and I adore...

Mr. President, in this cursed and sacred place you are facing your greatest audience. Here you stand in the presence of four million innocent souls. In their name, and with the authority of the number engraved on my arm, I say to you that if they could answer your noble words they would cry out: "Never again!" Never again between Frenchman and German, between Turk and Greek, between Indian and Pakistani. Never again between Arab and Jew. In their name I thank you for your pilgrimage to this shrine of martyrdom and agony. Your gesture inspires universal hope that the statesmen of the world will pay new heed to the clouds of violence that are gathering around us. That they will spare no effort to lead us to a safer and better future.
(*Bialystoker Memorial Book*, p. 200.)

When Samuel Pisar died at age 86 in 2015, an obituary summarized his story:

Mr. Pisar had an extraordinary life that arced from Bialystok, where he was born on March 18, 1929, through the Nazi death camps, and on to education in Australia, at Harvard and at the Sorbonne. He was 10 when Poland was swallowed by Hitler and Stalin. He somehow survived the camps of Majdanek, Auschwitz and Dachau, emerging at 16, hardened and wild, his family gone to ash....In a series of interviews with The New York Times in 2009, he described how he had survived the death camps by becoming pitiless and cruel... He was condemned to die at least twice, but managed to slip back into the general prison population, once convincing a guard that he was there only to wash the floor. "I had to learn bad habits," he said, "to be good at lying and make instant judgments about people, what they were saying, what they really thought, and not just the guards and torturers, but my fellow prisoners, too. I was a cute kid, and there were a lot of psychotics around." At the end of the war, he escaped during a death march. But to rejoin the world, "I had to wipe out the first 17 years of my life," he said. "I muted the past" and "turned to the future with a vengeance."

Years later, having been pressed by his wife's friend Leonard Bernstein, Mr. Pisar, like Job, took his arguments to God. Mr. Bernstein, always unhappy with the lyrics of the "Kaddish" Symphony No. 3 he wrote in 1963 that was dedicated to the assassinated President Kennedy, asked Mr. Pisar to write them instead. Pisar refused, feeling that his talents were not equal to the music, but after Bernstein's death, in 1990, and prompted by the terrorist attacks of Sept. 11, Mr. Pisar finally accepted the task, writing a version of the Kaddish, the Jewish prayer for the dead, that was first performed in 2003 with the Chicago Symphony Orchestra. A highlight for Mr. Pisar was the ability to perform his Kaddish in Israel in 2009 to a hushed audience at Yad Vashem, the Holocaust museum. The concert was a memorial to the victims of the Warsaw ghetto, and to his daughter it was also a sort of homecoming. "It was so much more resonant there than elsewhere," she said. "It was as if he was saying Kaddish for all the six million. (NY Times, July 28, 2015.)

9

Two Poles Who Were
Haunted By Jewish Voices

Jerzy Ficowski (1924-2006) was a Polish intellectual who displayed empathy for Poland's persecuted Jews and gypsies (Roma). During the war he fought in the underground Home Army and participated in the Warsaw Uprising. Ficowski found his poetic voice after the war ended, but with the government under Soviet influence his works were censored. It wasn't until 1979 that his collection of 27 poems called *Odczytanie popiolow* (A Reading of Ashes) finally was published and praised as the most moving depiction of the Holocaust ever written by a non-Jew or, as he once described himself, "I, their unburnt brother."

When Jerzy Ficowski began this project in about 1950, one poem was given the unusual title *Letter to Marc Chagall*. It's unclear why the unknown young poet chose to address the famous painter in this way - a man whom he'd never met. Some two decades later (1971) Ficowski recalled that he'd often admired Chagall's scenes of Jewish figures floating in the sky, but that in the context of the Holocaust they no longer could be understood merely as pretty or romantic pictures: "In a way, they [Chagall's floating lovers] descended into an inhuman time, associating themselves with the ashes of the crematoria."

However, as Ficowski described years later in a magazine article ("The Story of a Letter", *POLAND*, March 1971) he had developed writer's block: "The poem just would not grow...the words withdrew, as if they were afraid that they would not express the content they were to carry." Unable to find a way to adequately express his feelings, Ficowski put the Chagall "letter" aside until some five years later when a book was published in Poland that contained transcripts of testimony made by young survivors of the Warsaw Ghetto. Nothing could so authentically express tragedy as these children's words, they burned into his soul and, newly inspired, Jerzy Ficowski decided to incorporate excerpts from these transcripts into several of his poems.

One of the poems published in *A Reading of Ashes* that was titled "The Seven Words" began, "Mummy! But I've been good! It's dark!" Those were the tragic last words of a child being shut in a gas chamber at Belzec as told by the only surviving prisoner. In several other poems Ficowski described a six year old ghetto girl by the name of Rose (Raisl) Gold whom he'd seen begging on a Warsaw street. Her voice haunted him: "So she cried...so she fell silent...so she died." Rose Gold's words also opened *Letter to Marc Chagall*:

> *Brother went out in the night, drank water from a puddle and died. We buried him at night in the wood. Once uncle went out of the bunker and never came back. We could not walk at all and even now we have weak legs. And Rose is always sad, she often cries and will not play with the children.*

Next Ficowski addressed Chagall directly, this time employing some of the artist's familiar images:

> *What a good thing, Sir, you do not know Rose Gold!*
> *The bunch of lilacs the lovers lie in would go up in smoke.*
> *The green musician's fiddle would cut his throat.*
> *The graveyard gate would turn to dust or be overgrown with brick.*
> *Paint would char the canvases.*
> *For the last, most terrible cry is always only silence.*

Jerzy Ficowski mailed a copy of his poem to Chagall who then was living in Provence and received a polite thank you note. But about a decade later, the poet received a surprise package from a Parisian publisher of 120 etchings by Chagall for him to co-sign. It seems that Chagall had entirely forgotten about the "letter" until in 1967 he heard on French radio a performance of a symphonic accompaniment to Ficowski's poem that had been written in 1961 by Polish composer Stanislaw Wiechowicz. It was broadcast by the Israel Philharmonic on a special program celebrating Warsaw's Ghetto Uprising. Listening to this Chagall was profoundly moved and decided to compose a visual accompaniment to illustrate Ficowski's words. But now, in addition to the familiar fiddlers, animals and lovers, there were burning buildings, billowing smoke, tombstones and corpses lying on the ground or floating in the air.

(Permission to reproduce Chagall's etching: copyright © 2019 Artists Rights Society (ARS), New York / ADAGP, Paris)

Although distracted by other major projects, Chagall eventually produced five untitled etchings (one is reproduced here) that were printed in a limited folio edition by the Maeght gallery in Paris. The words of the ghetto children had inspired literary, musical and graphic responses and, in effect, Ficowski's poem and Chagall's etchings were requiems for victims of the Holocaust. Each man in his own way was venting rage and expressing frustration at their impotence and it's been suggested that Jerzy Ficowski may have been messaging in his collection of poems that "reading ashes" can lead to remembrance - and, if so, perhaps as testament to the resilience and eventual revival of the Jewish people.

Tomek Wisniewski was born in 1958 and moved with his family to Bialystok when he was seventeen years old. While attending Warsaw University he became a political dissident and in 1982 was arrested and spent nine months in jail. During that period government censorship limited what books could be read in public libraries but that wasn't the case in prison libraries. By chance, Tomek found a book in prison that described the Bialystok ghetto and the almost total annihilation of Poland's Jewish population. This changed his outlook about his town, his country, even his own identity and he decided to learn whatever he could about Jewish life in Bialystok before the war.

Like most of his generation Tomek had no inkling that his native city once was an important center of Jewish life. He was unaware that Jews made up the majority of Bialystok's pre-war population, nor that in 1941 the Nazis herded roughly 1,000 Jews into the city's main synagogue and then torched the building. After he was released from prison, Tomek asked scholars whether these things were true and was told they were but it was forbidden to talk about or teach them because it was against communist doctrine. Banned from many jobs because of his history of dissidence, Tomek persuaded a local newspaper to print brief articles about the city's Jewish history. When he began investigating pre-war guides and newspapers it felt as if he was discovering a lost world that had vanished from view, drowned like the mythical continent of Atlantis. In fact, the title of a series of more than one hundred short articles he wrote for the newspaper was "Postcards from Atlantis."

As Tomek described: "I tried to tell the story of what before the war was practically a Jewish city. But then, elderly people and even a few Jews began to seek me out at the news office. I talked with them for hours and taped these conversations, I roamed throughout the city; they showed me the buildings of old pre-war Jewish schools. At the same time, I read, read, read, all that I could get my hands on about this subject. And so it began. I made contacts with Jews from Bialystok in Israel, the USA, Australia, everywhere. They sent me their books, photocopies of documents and photographs."

For more than three decades Tomek has devoted his life to preserving Jewish history in the Bialystok region. He published books and articles, collected nearly two thousand vintage postcards and photographs, curated exhibitions and produced more than four hundred short documentary films. He studied Hebrew in order to be able to translate inscriptions on tombstones and preserve them for posterity. Tomek set up a web site, a virtual museum, that includes thousands of historic photographs of cemeteries, synagogues and other heritage sites. Hardly a Jewish visitor on an ancestry trip to the Bialystok region has not read, met or been guided by Tomek, but when praised for his work, he protests that he's no hero: "I do what I'm supposed to do."

In 1998 Tomek Wisniewski was one of the first recipients of an annual award presented by the State of Israel to honor non-Jewish Poles who care about Jewish heritage in Poland. Two decades later, at a gala event in Warsaw on December 4, 2018, he received the prestigious main prize of the POLIN Museum in Warsaw for contributions "to both the revival of the memory of the Polish Jews and building mutual understanding and respect between Poles and Jews." As Tomek said, "The history of the Jews of Bialystok is not just Jewish history for me. The history of the Jews in Bialystok and of Polish Jews in general is a major part of Polish history. Poles who deny themselves knowledge of this history remain ignorant of themselves and their past. They never get to know who they really are. It is they who are the losers, nobody else."

Once when asked what Poland would be like if there'd been no Holocaust, Tomek Wisniewski replied, "No doubt it would be troubled by the same problems and conflicts that afflict any multi-cultural society.

Michael Nevins

Some people would nurse anti-Jewish prejudices while others would practice the centuries-old traditions of Polish tolerance. One priest might inveigh against the Jews from the pulpit, while another might spend his evenings in the company of the local rabbi merrily drinking a glass of kosher altar wine and chatting away in a land in which 'holocaust' would be just a word."

10

Epilogue

When Dr. Ludwig Zamenhof (1859-1917) was a child growing up in Bialystok, Jews constituted nearly two thirds of the city's population. There was much conflict between ethnic and religious groups and, as he would recall, "In Bialystok the population consisted of four diverse elements: Russians, Poles, Germans and Jews; each spoke a different language and was hostile to the other elements...The diversity of languages is the only, or at least the main cause, that separates the human family and divides it into conflicting groups. I was brought up as an idealist; I was taught that all men were brothers and, meanwhile, in the streets, in the square, everything made me feel that men did not exist, only Russians, Poles, Germans and Jews and so on." Bialystok was a virtual Tower of Babel and the precocious high school student resolved to do something about it, inventing the international language Esperanto in 1887 as a way of promoting world peace, justice and goodwill. Esperanto means "Hope" and although Zamenhof's utopianism failed to achieve its goal, one way of combatting hatred is involves language by hearing and heeding the words of its victims.

Historian Lawrence Langer concluded his scholarly analysis *Holocaust Testimonies* by noting that from the raw material of individual narratives, "a kind of unshielded truth emerges through which we salvage an anatomy of melancholy for the modern spirit...For the former victims [and survivors], the Holocaust is a communal wound that cannot heal....

When the subtext of their story echoes for us too as a communal wound, then we will have begun to hear their legacy of unheroic memory and grasp the meaning for our time of a diminished self." (L. Langer, p. 204)

Although David Spiro's voice was cut off early, his story and those of others like him should be remembered. Their words provide new ways for us to understand matters we thought we already knew all about. Now that David's diary has been saved from oblivion, let us pay attention and learn from it. Yes, words matter!

ACKNOWLEDGEMENTS

The cover art and four interior illustrations for this book were made by Mark Podwal whose mother was born in Dabrowa Bialostocka. After visiting his ancestral shtetl in 2016, Podwal was inspired to produce what he called a "visual diary" of the trip. Afterward it was published by the Yiddish Book Center and widely exhibited as *Kaddish for Dabrowa Bialostocka*. The drawings that are included here were created for a documentary film produced by Tomek Wisniewski about the destruction of the Bialystok Synagogue.

I am especially grateful to Jolanta Szczygiel-Rogowska and David Bujno of the Slendzinski Gallery in Bialystok for permission to reproduce lengthy edited extracts from *Pamiętnik* (David Spiro's Diary) that in 2016 was published in Polish with English translation by Konrad Pormanczuk. Historian Wieslaw Wrobel did extensive research about the Szpiro family for that edition while Dr. Michel Bodkier of Bordeaux contributed genealogical information about Szpiro family descendants. Historians Aleksandra Bankowska and Weronika Romanik provided details about the Mersik-Tenenbaum Archive and Mordecai's manifesto.

Portions of Sara Bender's book *The Jews of Bialystok. During World War II and the Holocaust From The Jews of Bialystock during World War II* were reprinted by permission of Brandeis University Press. Limited materials from *The Bialystoker Memorial Book* were approved by the Yizkor Book Project of *JewishGen*.

Special thanks to Elzbieta Smolenska who introduced me to David Spiro's diary, made many useful suggestions and helped coordinate this project. My thanks also go to Tomek Wisniewski, authority in all things related to Bialystok Jewry, for permitting me to describe his personal story.

NOTES

1. In November 1939 Chiune "Sempo" Sugihara, a Japanese career diplomat, was sent to Kovno (Kaunas), then the capital of Lithuania, to serve as Japan's Vice-Consul. Starting in July 1940, Sugihara helped as many as six thousand Jews flee Europe by issuing transit visas so they could travel through Japanese territory to Curacao. Sugihara worried about official reaction to the thousands of visas he issued but many years later he recalled, "No one ever said anything about it. I remember thinking that they probably didn't realize how many I actually issued." In a personal communication to me genealogist Mark Halpern noted that there's suggestive but inconclusive evidence that David Spiro's's father Pinchas may have been among about 1,500 Jews who reached Kobe Japan. At the onset of World War II, that enclave was transferred to Japanese-held Shanghai where approximately 30,000 Jews were confined in a ghetto. When that community dissolved after the war, Pinchas Szpiro's name was not on emigration lists kept by the American Jewish Joint Distribution Committee and, like with his son David, his fate is unknown.

2. More detail can be found in Bronka Klibanski's "The Underground Archives of the Bialystok Ghetto Founded by Mersik and Tenenbaum," *Yad Vashem Studies 2* (1958) 295-329 and Sara Bender's *The Jews of Bialystok*. Also, a review of the archival holdings written by Aleksandra Bankowska can be found on the website of the U.S. Historical Memorial Museum.

3. During the first days of the Warsaw Ghetto Uprising in April 1943, a similar manifesto was issued there by the Jewish Armed Resistance Organization:

> *Poles, citizens, soldiers of Freedom! Through the din of German canons, destroying the homes of our mothers, wives and children; through the noise of machine guns, seized by us in the fight against the cowardly German police and SS men; through the smoke of the Ghetto that was set on fire, and the blood of its mercilessly killed defenders, we, the slaves of the Ghetto, convey heartfelt greetings to you. We are well aware that you have been witnessing breathlessly with broken hearts, with tears of compassion, with horror and enthusiasm, the war that we have been waging against the brutal occupant these past few days....Every footstep in the Ghetto has become a stronghold and shall remain a fortress until the end! All of us will probably perish in the fight, but we shall never surrender! We, as well as you, are burning with desire to punish the enemy for all his crimes with a desire for vengeance, It is a fight for freedom, as well as yours; for our human dignity and national honor, as well as yours! We shall avenge the gory deeds of Oswiecim, Treblinka, Belzec and Majdanek!....Long live the fraternity of blood and weapons in a fighting Poland! Long live freedom! Death to the hangmen and the killer! We must continue our mutual struggle against the occupant until the very end!*
> (M. Edelman. pp. 77-78.)

4. After the Russians liberated Bialystok, a memorial event was held to honor those who'd perished and a new library was dedicated in Pesach Kaplan's name. It contained 2,000 books donated by former residents in the United States and Argentina and 200 more contributed by a single ethnic Pole who'd been entrusted with them by his Jewish neighbors. Today Pesach Kaplan's two diaries are preserved in the archives of Yad Vashem.

5. Chaika Grossman was decorated with Poland's highest decoration of valor, the Grunwald Cross. When she emigrated to Palestine in 1948, she informed the Zionist leadership and those who'd left Poland before the war about the slaughter of their families and friends. Seven months after she made *aliyah* she wrote her memoir *People of the Underground* in Hebrew. It detailed her life as a ghetto courier, organizer and fighter but Haika wasn't satisfied. Two years earlier when she'd visited the United States as a member of a group representing Polish Jewry, she was disturbed that although the people she met were extremely sympathetic, they didn't fully understand what had happened. It wasn't until an expanded English edition of her memoir was published in 1987 that her perspective on events was fully explained for an American audience.

Chaika Grossman was elected to the Knesset where she focused on social issues and the status of women. In 1993 Prime Minister Yitzhak Rabin invited her to join his entourage in a journey to Warsaw to commemorate the 50th anniversary of the ghetto revolt. On the day of her return home, Chaika lit one of twelve torches traditionally kindled on Mount Herzl in Jerusalem celebrating the 45th year of independence of the State of Israel. Later that evening at a party at the villa of Sheik Muhamad, she gave a speech saying, "I am pleased that as a former Member of Knesset and a Holocaust survivor, I was given the opportunity to ignite a beacon together with an Arab who has tied his destiny with the State of Israel. I hear the sound of peace approaching." Sadly at the end of the party, Chaika slipped while going down a steep stairway, hit her head and lapsed into a coma from which she never fully recovered; she died three years later.

SOURCES

Bankowska, Aleksandra. "Inventory of the Underground Archives of the Bialystok Archives (Mersik-Tenenbaum) 1941-1943." *Archives of the Jewish Historical Science and Research Institute,* Warsaw. RG-15.150. 2009. 143

Bender, Sara. *The Jews of Bialystok. During World War II and the Holocaust.* Brandeis University Press, 2008. (Permission to reproduce portions by Brandeis University Press.)

Bialystoker Memorial Book, The. The Bialystoker Center. New York: Empire Press, 1982. Edited by I. Shmulewitz. (Permission to reproduce portions from JewishGen. Yizkor Book Project.)

Edelman, Marek. *The Ghetto Fights. Warsaw 1943-45.* London: Bookmarks. 2014.

Ficowski, Jerzy. *A Reading of Ashes.* London: The Menard Press. 1981.

Garbarini, Alexandra. *Numbered Days. Diaries and the Holocaust.* New Haven:Yale University Press, 2006

Gessen, Masha. *Two Babushkas.* London, Bloomsbury, 2004

Grossman, Chaika. *The Underground Army. Fighters of the Bialystok Ghetto.* New York: Holocaust Library, 1987. (Hebrew edition published in Israel in 1965.)

Kassow, Samuel D. *Who will write our history? Rediscovering a Hidden Archive from the Warsaw Ghetto.* New York: Random House, Inc. 2009.

Klibanski-Winicki, Bronia. *Ariadne.* Tel Aviv: Geranium Publishers, 2002. Reviewed at www.haretz.com/life/books/1.5094824

Klibanski, Bronia. "The Underground Archives of the Bialystok Ghetto Founded by Mersik and Tenenbaum," *Yad Vashem Studies* 2(1958) 295-329.

Kobrin, Rebecca. *Jewish Bialystok and Its Diaspora*. Bloomington: Indiana University Press, 2010.

Langer, Lawrence. *Holocaust Testimonies. the ruins of memory*. New Haven: Yale University Press, 1991.

Lew, Henry R. *Lion Hearts. A Family Saga of Refugees and Asylum Seekers*. Melbourne: Hybrid Publishers, 2012.

Pisar, Samuel. *Of Blood and Hope*. New York: MacMillan. 1979.

Rozenberg, Lena Jedwab. *Girl with Two Landscapes. The Wartime Diary of Lena Jedwab, 1941-1945*. New York: Holmes & Meier, 2002.

Schor, Esther. "Esperanto - A Jewish Story." *Pakn Treger*. Winter 2009, No. 60.

Sheraton, Mimi. *The Bialy Eaters*. New York: Broadway Books, 2000.

Spiegel, Renia. *Renia's Diary*. New York: St. Martin's Press, 2019

Wisniewski, Tomasz. *Jewish Bialystok and Surroundings in Eastern Poland*. Ipswitch, MA: The Ipswich Press, 1998.

Zable, Arnold. *Jewels and Ashes*. New York: Harcourt Brace & Comp. 1991.

Zabuski, Charles "Shleimah". *Needle and Thread. A Tale of Survival from Bialystok to Paris*. Oakland: Popincourt Press, 1996

Zapruder, Alexandra. *Salvaged Pages: Young Writers' Diaries of the Holocaust*, Second Edition. New Haven: Yale University Press, 2015.